Amanda Prantera was born and educated in England, where she studied philosophy as a research student  She now lives in Rome, and is married with two c

Her first novel, *Strange Loop*, v wide critical acclaim. It is also availab

Also by Amanda Prantera in Abacus:

STRANGE LOOP

Amanda Prantera
The Cabalist

First published in Great Britain by
Jonathan Cape Ltd 1985
Published in Abacus by
Sphere Books Ltd 1987
27 Wrights Lane, London W5 5TZ
Copyright © 1985 by Amanda Prantera

Set in Linotron Palatino

Printed and bound in great Britain by
Collins, Glasgow

To my mother
and my daughters

I

'Mr . . .'; THE doctor paused and had a quick look at his notes, the subject being inescapably personal. 'Mr Keller. Sorry. Mr Kestler. You have no living relatives then, is that right? No brother? No sister? A close friend perhaps . . .?' He paused again on a hopeful note as if he thought his patient might possess decisional powers over these facts. 'In a case like this it is often helpful to keep in contact with members of the family as well, you know. Not merely helpful – essential, really.'

Joseph nodded sympathetically. The surgeon was much younger than he was, with freckles and a tidy, shovel-shaped beard, and he would have liked to have been able to help him out of his quandary. Although living so out of step with his times as to have no idea what a classic quandary it was, he knew exactly what it consisted of: he had some fatal disease or other (judging by all the coughing he was doing nowadays and by the number of X-rays they had seen fit to bombard his chest with, he thought it was most probably cancer of the lung), and the doctor could neither tell him this outright nor allow him to leave without telling him in a more roundabout way. It was a tricky problem indeed. A dilemma. The doctor's dilemma, though. His death, but the doctor's dilemma.

There seemed no way to put a comfortable end to the interview (which, anyway, he thought after a surreptitious glance at his watch, had lasted quite long enough for both parties) other than to take an energetic dive between the horns of the dilemma – a standard technique, if he remembered rightly, much recommended by all important texts on rhetoric. When he did so, however, the doctor's embarrassment seemed if anything to grow.

'Cancer?' he echoed with poorly feigned surprise. 'Now why should you think a thing like that, Mr Keller? Kestler? That won't do at all. No, it won't do at all to have you go imagining a thing like that. When I mentioned the importance of contacting your relatives it was just to enlist a little extra help over your treatment. These medicines I have prescribed need taking regularly, you know, and two heads are better than one in such cases. They may tend to upset you a bit too – a touch of nausea, slight loss of appetite – nothing serious, of course. And when you come in for your checks it would be a comfort for you to have someone to accompany you home.'

'I see,' said Joseph thoughtfully. Treatment, the doctor called it. There was to be no surgery, and he was being issued with prescriptions for analgesics and morphine. That didn't sound much like treatment to him, however generously you stretched the word; it sounded more like throwing in the sponge.

He bypassed the worried gaze of the doctor, leaving him for a moment to founder alone on the ethical niceties of his profession, and looked out of the window beyond him at the shimmering fabric of darkness, brightness and water. It was getting late. Late in the day and late – so very much later than he had suspected – in his life. However, there was such a lot of work still to be done that he could hardly afford to let this upset him. He put his hands under the desk where the doctor could not see them and began methodically ticking off on his fingers the main headings of the important questions which needed tying up before he could quit the world in peace with his own conscience; each of which, taken singly, would under normal conditions take him days if not weeks of industry. Finish rereading (in case there was something of vital importance in the works of the others which had escaped him); commit his own work – his secret, his message to the world – to tidy and legible writing; sound out Trevisan to see if he could be entrusted with its safe-keeping; and, on the side (seeing that no one else would be likely to bother about this when he was gone), do something about the obnoxious Catcher. Four fingers. Four principal activities. Four things that could not be left undone. Summed up like that on the fingers of just one hand it did not seem too overwhelming a task. Not if he could draw up a programme and set about things in an orderly way. Fifth point then, he muttered to himself resolutely, bunching his thumb to the rest of the fingers; fifth point: draw up a working timetable.

Of course, for a proper schedule it would be helpful to know roughly how much time he had left, but he very much doubted the doctor would tell him this now, even if he could. He had already violated the man's canons of professional delicacy quite rudely enough. He had mentioned death, had given his disease the blunt name of cancer, and in this he had unwittingly made such a grave breach of taste that it was unlikely he would be allowed to make another. Still, the matter was of such extreme importance to him that he must try. He spread his fingers wide again, drummed them in absent-minded rhythm against the underside of the desk and awaited an opportunity to make a second dive.

With a silent flurry a seagull came to rest on the window-sill behind the doctor's shoulders and began to preen its feathers, giving the impression that it was on a plane with him and was nibbling at his beard. Joseph smiled; it made a very engaging picture – the serious face of the doctor with the bird nestling alongside it and burrowing industriously at its contours. A pity he didn't know more names of birds. Or more names of anything for that matter. It made him wonder for a moment, in a small, bleak hiatus of confidence, whether his heritage – the fund of knowledge he had taken a lifetime to sift and to amass and which it was now his duty to hand down to posterity – was such an important one after all. At present all he could vouch for was a limitedly manipulative power over raindrops and locusts. Not a great deal in an age when researchers in other fields had learnt how to blast their planet to baldness, or how to abandon it altogether for a stroll on the surface of the moon. Still, he comforted himself on second reflection, it was the principle behind the thing that mattered. As with all discoveries in their early stages, it was the theory which was important, not the present range of its use. And it was surely a sound enough theory, since not only could you verify it and make sure that it worked, but (what people nowadays seemed to think more important) you could falsify it as well and see that it didn't. What more could you ask of a theory? Yes, he would have to be very quick about finishing his testament and very careful about whose hands he left it in.

The doctor was scratching at the opposite side of his beard to the seagull and saying something to him now in a low, unhappy voice about symptoms. From his words Joseph could picture his own lungs nestling somewhere inside his frame like a pair of run-down and corroded batteries. He smiled again, this time in polite acknowledgment. In a way it was interesting to learn which piece of the machinery was to be responsible for the extinction of the rest. That much at least the science of medicine could tell him. It did not seem to be able to tell him frankly whether or not he was going to die – ridiculous, he thought crossly, when there could surely be little doubt as to the answer to *that* – nor did it seem to want to tell him when, but it could at least tell him on what account. So it was to be the lungs. Not the heart, as he had suspected when the pain set in, but cancer of the lungs. Ah well. Location apart, it didn't really surprise him much. After all, it was in the nature of things. In fact, from an unbiased viewpoint he supposed it was really something of a conquest for the species to have a succession of separate individuals replacing one another and renewing one another's energy, rather than to have the same tired brains ticking on for ever in the same tired bodies. That was where the beauty of the chain came in. He must fulfil his role as link, work as hard and as long as the failing batteries would feed him, and then surrender the strain and allow it to be taken up by the next link.

He shifted uneasily on his chair. The trouble was that unbiasedness was not that easy to achieve for someone in his position and with his responsibilities. Not only was there posterity to be considered, but his forerunners as well. And to be true to them, to set the seal of utility on the centuries and centuries of collective research, it was just not enough that he should have succeeded in cracking the riddle. Not unless there was someone, somewhere, prepared not only to believe him but to undertake to carry on the great work. Someone, somewhere, sometime, bearing a torch that his tiny ember of hard-won knowledge could ignite. If no successor could be found at present – and his whole way of life, devoted as it had been to study and to solitude, had given him very little chance even to start looking for one – then he must fall swiftly back on the expedient of putting his knowledge down in writing and of consigning it to someone he could trust. Which was where Trevisan came in. Study; clean-copying; Trevisan to win round; and some scheme to devise for blocking or hampering the Catcher. What a lot still to be done, he thought wearily, and under what prohibitive conditions. It would come in very handy to have at least a rough idea of the time that remained.

He shifted again impatiently on the hard plastic of the seat and looked at the gull. The bird's sleek shape stood out with luminous whiteness against the watery backcloth; it was getting very late indeed.

Cutting across the subdued, professional voice of the doctor which had been purring on for some time now in a detailed blend of pseudo-explanation and advice to which he had been able to grant only a very small amount of attention, he asked gently: 'Is there any way of gauging how long this . . . illness of mine will last?'

'*Mister* . . . er . . . Kestler,' replied the doctor sternly, the effort of keeping his patience in the face of such wilful disattention causing him to screw his eyes tight shut and to draw in his breath with an abrupt hiss; 'Mr Kestler,' he repeated more kindly, opening them again and studying Joseph with genuine bewilderment, 'have you been listening to what I was saying?' Joseph nodded obediently in answer and composed his face, only a shade too late, to gravity.

'Well then, you will have realized – in fact, I have only just finished explaining this to you – that an incurable disease, although not necessarily *cancer* and not necessarily an *untreatable* disease, is most emphatically a disease which will last as long as you do yourself. Which may, of course,' he added hastily, 'indeed in all probability in your case *will*, be a considerable length of time yet.'

'That's just it,' put in Joseph mildly. 'Perhaps I should have put it the other way round. What I really want to know is how long *I* will last. Or, if you prefer it, how long will we both last – the disease and I together. It is a question of my work,' he added with sudden inspiration, managing to check yet another burst of impatience on the doctor's part by allowing an authentic touch of urgency to infect his words. 'The work I am engaged on is very important.'

'Ah,' said the doctor in a changed tone, lowering his eyes respectfully and consulting the papers before him. 'You are . . . now what does it say here? Ah, yes. Here we are. You are an interpreter, is that right?'

Joseph, although he could not remember having given him this piece of information himself, thought that it summed up very nicely the rather fuzzy and disparate natures of his various professions. 'I am,' he confirmed.

'Hmm, yes, well, Mr Kestler,' resumed the doctor on a sanguine but less respectful note, rubbing his hands pliantly together and then setting about drilling his papers into a well-matched rectangle; 'now I think you need have no fears on that score. You may find yourself obliged to cut down your working hours a little – to take things a bit easier than you have in the past. But there is no call at this stage for you to worry unduly about your work. As I was trying to explain to you before, although the right paratracheal soft-tissue spaces are a trifle on the wide side . . .'

Joseph listened politely, his head tilted to one side, following the tidying-up process with admiration (for in his own experience, papers were not usually so amenable to discipline), and waiting for an opportunity to take his leave. As he had feared, the timetable would have to be a rather vague one, and remain open-ended.

It was interesting though, he mused as he waited, to see how the fellow had faltered there for just that one instant. It showed that there were categories of patients (interpreters, evidently, not among them) who were allowed still a certain dignity, even in the consulting-room. Interesting. Businessmen, maybe, he thought vaguely. Managers, perhaps. Executives, whatever they might be. He ought, of course, to have said that he was an executive. That was it. And it would have been quite correct too, in a manner of speaking. He *was* an executive after all – very definitely so. Now, not all his predecessors could truthfully have said the same of themselves, although *some* undoubtedly could have. A faint chuckle escaped him as he pictured to himself one of these majestic figures from the past sitting there in his place, brandishing a fist in the face of the discomforted doctor (and small wonder he was discomforted, Joseph told himself tolerantly, pitted as he was against an invisible enemy whom he considered it impolite to name or even to acknowledge); sitting there – or maybe standing, for they would never have put up with these dreadful plastic chairs – and claiming their right to know. None of them, surely, even though it be further allowed that in their days it had been a topic with a touch of dash about it, had ever been ashamed of death? Not that he was ashamed of himself, exactly; but he certainly did not cut a very majestic figure. Another consequence, this, he supposed, of the lopsidedness of twentieth-century medicine – of its being so powerful over some things yet so helpless over others, and possessing knowledge so detailed as to the whys and wherefores, yet so scrappy as to the ifs and whens. It was hard indeed to keep your dignity, let alone majesty, once a doctor had seen right into you and had set his eyes on the sorry spectacle of your two decaying batteries of lungs. Whichever way you looked at it (in fact, precisely *because* you had looked at it every which way), there was no dash about tar-filled pleura, and nothing at all heroic about a pair of dwindling batteries. They merely spelled defeat to the man of medicine, and to himself the simple but inescapable fact that he would shortly be making an exit from the world for want of energy: a routine event, he supposed, however unwelcome to him personally, but one which must on no account take place until he was ready for it.

It was dark when he left the clinic and made his way back to his lodgings. The doctor had been worried but rather glad to see him go, for, as Joseph himself fully realized, he had not been an easy patient to deal with. True, he had done his best to cover up this failure by promising to keep in touch, had written the doctor's telephone number dutifully on the back of his hand where he could be sure not to mislay it, and to the consultant's evident relief, had murmured something about moving shortly to another city to continue treatment there; but he had not been an easy patient. On leaving, he had screwed the carefully written prescriptions, together with instructions for dosage, into a tight little ball (he could not *possibly*, he had whispered sternly to himself, risk furring up his brain with morphine and stuff like that), and had flicked it into a nearby canal. This he had done so promptly that he half feared the doctor might still have been watching. He hoped not. It would only have unsettled the poor fellow further, and might too have had the undesired effect of leaving a mark on his memory, when Joseph so very earnestly did not want to be remembered by him. Not just now at any rate. Few people had watched him living, and he wished for fewer still to watch him dying. He did not even want to watch himself, as far as he could manage it. He wanted to forget all about it and to concentrate on more pressing matters.

Before turning to such matters, however, he granted himself one last reflection on the theme, and a consoling one at that; noting with a certain pride that he had chosen, if not the time, at least the place with foresight. You could, after all, with nothing more than a little spirit of adventure in your make-up, live in many spots, but the place of your death had about it the same kind of capricious uniqueness as that of your birth. He was . . . not glad exactly – that would be an ungrateful way of putting it – but satisfied that his was to be here. Were it not for the fight against time, he might almost prefer the event to take place before the spring when the tourist season started, so that at such a crucial moment he could have the beloved city a little more to himself. Although on the other hand, if he did last out until the spring, then it would mean he would have time not only to finish his work without rushing, but also to wander round a little – strength permitting – and pay a few brief farewell visits to his most favourite places. So either way things would not turn out too badly. He could take a boat to the islands again; he could spend the afternoon watching the birds skim over the lagoon; he could sit on the jetty of San Francesco del Deserto in the setting sunshine and watch the tracery of the trees against the vanishing horizon; he could settle himself comfortably down on the last bench of the Dogana and enjoy the bustling exertion of the rowers training for their next regatta, or have a little chat with the groups of very young and very old fishermen who gathered there companionably on Sundays and never bothered him by catching anything.

He could do all this again if he was given the time; and if he wasn't, then he could work hard and fast and make his exit in the quiet of winter. No, no, neither alternative was too bleak. For a start he could also cancel all his other work. The tiresome business – ever jarring against his true interests – of earning enough to keep alive, could now safely be set aside. What money he had would see him through. That, in fact, was a positively pleasing prospect, and he must remember to get busy about it tomorrow. He must also remember to stop in at the bar on his way back and call Trevisan to arrange a meeting (and while he was about it, perhaps he had better suggest a meal, as it might make the conversation a little less awkward), since there was the pressing matter of custody to be tackled. Ideally, of course, what he would like would be to get Trevisan to winkle the testament into the University for him – if they would accept it, that was – or, failing this, into some other responsible sort of institution; but in order to grant the work a double guarantee of safety he would also like him to retain his role of custodian, and keep an eye on it from a distance. It was essential, therefore, thoroughly to assess his honesty and integrity. Or rather (since their long

15

and untroubled acquaintance was, he supposed, proof of these virtues to some extent) to delve deeper and plumb the purity of his heart. No easy matter, over the supper-table. What use, if any, for example, would a suddenly powerful Trevisan wish to make of his newly acquired faculty? How far could he be trusted not to abuse it? How much was it necessary to tell him? Was the humility he possessed of a suitably steady variety? Was he strong enough? Again, did he believe – really and truly believe – in an objective standard of goodness? It was funny how you could know a person so long without knowing to any degree of certainty these fundamental facts about him. And how, Joseph wondered, could he set about finding them out now, at such a late date and with so little time at his disposal? Come to think of it, he did not even know whether Trevisan believed in God.

Riffling carefully through these questions in his mind and lining up alongside them a tentative list of solutions, he turned up the collar of his mackintosh against the rain and plodded off determinedly to the nearest point of embarkation. It was late, and there was much to be done; but he had no doubt that he would manage somehow.

II

THE STAGE on which this story takes place, easily identified by the seagull, the canal and various other, more specific pointers, is Venice; which is, of course, a splendid place to stage anything. Splendid even as it is now on a cold and rainy autumn evening, raked by a wind so wet and so strong that it penetrates walls, windows, clothing and skin alike with a thoroughness no human outlay is able wholly to balk, whether it be outlay of money, of industry, of ingenuity or sheer straightforward luck. The rich may be a little drier than the poor, the cunning perhaps a little warmer than the gormless, and so forth, but it goes no further than that. Dampness dominates all. Her inhabitants on this particular evening, too, may seem more than usually dejected on this account and more than figuratively under the weather, but Venice herself is still indisputably splendid. More so than ever, in fact. For while by the harsher light of day she opens up her history and endures scrutiny in a passive, disarmed way (rather like an ageing beauty submitting for pragmatic reasons to examination by a dermatologist), when her imperfections are veiled by darkness or by mist she takes heart again, decks herself out in all her finery, and outspokenly courts attention – shining, sparkling and triumphantly seducing as in the days of her prime.

Tonight, what with rain and darkness, the veil is a double one and she is at it busily, only too aware of presenting herself to most judicious advantage. On her seaward front is set the Byzantine jewel of St Mark's, sombre and lustreless at this time of evening, squatting in the shadows like a huge dragonfly whose wings are furled. It lies there ponderously, massively, its bulk offset by the towers and spires of countless other, smaller churches which mirror themselves in sequin pattern on the surface of the water – slender, bright, and insubstantial as so many will-o'-the-wisps. The basilica, in fact, seems almost to have been put there as a kind of functional afterthought, to counterbalance the filigree lightness of the rest of the city, to weight it down and prevent it from taking flight. And through the very centre of all this dazzle the Grand Canal cuts its way, unfolding itself like a bolt of spangled silk between the rows of palaces on either bank, describing a curve as involved and arbitrary as the cutting of a jigsaw.

As the canal approaches its outlet into open waters, however, the palaces become progressively darker and more deserted; the delicacy of their pale, ribbed structures lending them a strange, spindly elegance that verges on the ghostly. They look more like skeletons now than buildings – very important skeletons, though, and very proud. And in their doorways static groups of gulls huddle together in unaccustomed silence, forming patches of whitish grey against the darkness, adding little spooky touches of their own. But even along this gloomier stretch, here and there an upper window glows with light, and the glimpse of a chandelier, a bookcase, or a pot of ivy with its leaves picked out in pointed silhouette, testifies that life within is not wholly extinct. Venice may be decaying, but she is still alive. Still alive and still resplendent, and providing a very sumptuous backcloth to our story.

The hero of the story, in contrast, has no visible traces of splendour whatever about his person, but is a small ageing man in a worn and by now redundant raincoat who is stepping off a vaporetto amidst a crowd of other passengers, mostly, like himself, soaked with rain, steaming off some residue of bodily heat, and on their way home from the labours of the day. He is hatless, umbrellaless, his collar is turned up in such a way that the rain is channelled directly on to the clothes beneath, and although he carries both a briefcase and a newspaper he uses neither to shield himself, nor yet the one to shield the other. Thus he is soggy and dripping, so is the briefcase, and so too is the newspaper. One is tempted by these facts to think that he is not well equipped in any of the commodities mentioned above and to sum him up quickly and with a fair dose of conviction as poor, unlucky and lacking in drive and resourcefulness. Not only on account of his clothing or wetness either; for there is also a tired, resigned air about him (something to do with the way he holds his head and shoulders, or the way he allows the other passengers to jostle past him in their illusory struggle towards shelter and dryness), which neither sunshine nor a change of wardrobe would seem capable of altering.

Immediate inference can, however, be misleading. He is, as a matter of fact, poor, and until recently he has been in many things unlucky; what is more, he has as we have seen just been served a piece of information sufficient to stun a less philosophically-minded person. But it will not do to dismiss his ingenuity out of hand since it may emerge shortly that he is rather well provided with it, although he doesn't seem to have put it to much use so far in his everyday life. He is certainly very industrious, very cultivated, and also has a kind, winning smile with a downward twitch to it, which, in the rare moments that he uses it, lights up his whole face and makes it twinkle. (Additions, you may object, that still seem to leave us with nothing more inspiring on our hands than an old, impecunious, failed and solitary intellectual with a nice smile, condemned very shortly to die.)

Anyway, before we go drawing any more wrong conclusions, it might be a good idea to follow him for a while as he ploughs his way across the wind-lashed square and makes for the relative comfort of his dwelling-place – he does not, and rightly, think of it as a home – to see if there is anything else in his appearance or behaviour that will help us to get to know him, or, more important, help us to discover what it is that singles him out from his fellow men and makes him interesting to the point of constructing a story around – apart, that is, from his own high opinion of his work, his gift for languages (he speaks half a dozen or so of these fluently, plus pretty good Italian), and his unfashionable attitude towards death.

For I assure you that he *is* interesting. There must be no doubt about this. He is very interesting indeed – be it for no other reason than that he practises a profession which would have set him apart from the rest of humanity had he lived in the Athens of Pericles, the France of Napoleon or the Chicago of Al Capone, but which in present-day Italy (nobody's Italy just now, but perhaps, who knows, one distant day to be referred to as his, Joseph Kestler's, very own Italy) sets him in such stark occupational isolation that he emerges not so much as a loner or an oddity but as a genuine, one-hundred-per-cent, dyed-in-the-wool freak. Nor is this all. For on account of this profession of his, and of the strange competence he has reached in it, he is about to find himself caught up in a very interesting, not to say dramatic, series of events. So perhaps, as the story goes on, I may be forgiven for choosing such a drab-looking hero and for saddling him from the start with the added handicap of mortal disease.

The crowd of passengers amongst whom he left the boat has now rapidly dispersed, leaving this slower and wetter member behind them. Walking measuredly across the square, side-stepping the puddles and giving an occasional toss of the head to free his spectacles from the rain, he takes an abrupt right turn under an arch and heads down a passageway scarcely wider than his shoulders, at the end of which there is a feeble patch of light. Here he negotiates a ramp of slippery steps, comes to a halt in front of a door so small and of such uniformly sodden texture to the walls that had we not been using him as a marker we should have passed it by unseeingly, and, after fumbling unhurriedly in his pockets for the key, lets himself in from the dark, wet night to the somewhat similar interior of his lodgings.

His landlady, bent over a long, thin, intricate piece of crochet work which she reels off skilfully by the sole light of a jaded and flickering television screen, seems unaffected by his arrival. Apart from a brief sniff of greeting and a burst of accelerated hookings of her thread, by which she manages to convey her disapproval of his wetness and the way he is dripping on to her already damp marble floor, she does not stir for him. If we compare this with the smiling 'Buona sera, Signora' which she produced only a few minutes earlier for her female lodger, whose money she will not accept unless wearing rubber gloves, and with the deferential shifting of weight from buttocks to feet with which she marked the arrival of the third (a middle-aged architectural student who pays his rent fitfully and practises on a wind instrument in his abundant spare time), we can see that poor Joseph is given a very low rating indeed. And this is significant, because landladies – particularly in Italy – are usually very accurate about the status of their boarders, and know to the millimetre how much respect is due to whom, and why. Whatever his particular genius consists in, therefore, it is presumably something he does on his own – if not in actual secret – and which has little or no overspill into his public life. Although, despite his discretion, one or two people in close contact with him may have some idea of what it is. There is Trevisan, for one, Joseph's chosen custodian, who in exchange for the odd game of cards helps him out every other Wednesday with the mathematical side of his work. He has at least an inkling, because Joseph cannot help opening up little pieces of his mind to him when they are going over some of the trickier points together. But since on these occasions Joseph is careful to keep the exposed pieces discrete (and not only the pieces of his mind, either, for he usually presents the doctor with incomplete pages of his research as well, cutting out the more revealing passages beforehand with scissors, or else pasting them over with squares of wrapping-paper and scotch tape), poor Trevisan's inkling remains rather vague. The more so, as he has never yet been nimble enough to take a peep under the squares without Joseph noticing. Anyway, is is high time we had a look inside the bedroom to dissipate the mystery for ourselves. We are nearly there now, for Joseph is groping his way down the unlighted corridor, relying for guidance on long habit and a sliver of light filtering from a neighbouring doorway.

'That you, Joe?' calls out a friendly male voice, in English seasoned with a thick Mediterranean accent. 'Yes,' replies Joseph quietly, without halting his steps, 'yes, I've just this moment got back.' 'Uhuh. Thought so. Thought it must be you,' says the voice, rounding off this last utterance with a sigh and a restrained belch. The voice, of course, belongs to the mature student, Emilio, and even from such a limited exchange it is clear that he is angling for conversation. He is probably lonely; or anxious to profit by Joseph's excellent English; or maybe both. But months of misfired effort in this direction have evidently taught him not to press too hard for his fellow lodger's company – particularly not at this time of day – and never to cross the threshold of his room unless invited, nor to keep him from whatever it is that he does there, evening after evening, for after a moment's silence, which Joseph is careful not to break, he merely gives another sigh and strikes up a laboured and melancholy scale on his basset horn without another word.

Joseph passes a second door, getting no greeting and giving none. His relationship to the lady behind it has become a little strained recently, although in this case it is she, not he, who is the stand-offish one. This third boarder, a trim, discreet prostitute of advanced years, known in the neighbourhood with curious use of antonomasia quite simply as 'the Signora' and much respected there, is in fact, counting Trevisan, the second person to date who has noticed that there is something strange about Joseph, something that does not quite tally with his public façade, and in her eyes it in no way constitutes a merit. She finds him weird; a bit unnerving. She is even a little frightened of him. For she has, you see, actually happened to see him at work. True, he was only practising and only on a very small scale, but she has chanced nevertheless to catch a clear glimpse of his particular ability and has since remained a bit worried by it. She keeps the thing very much to herself, though, for she is sensitive to public opinion and is afraid of being laughed at. Besides, at a distance of several months she is no longer very sure of what she did see when she poked her head round the door of his room that day without knocking and caught him at it. We also shall enter without knocking, following silently in the footsteps of Joseph himself.

The room is painted, or has once been painted, a pale, watery green, in keeping with the patches of humidity on the walls and with the small backwater branch of canal which stagnates some metres below the window, abob with orange peel, plastic bottles, lettuce leaves and various other bits of flotsam less easy to identify. Joseph has long learnt to accept the miscellany with interested tolerance, but he is less tolerant of the draught and the view, and on entering he goes straight to the window, tests it automatically to see if it is shut, and then pulls the grubby muslin curtain across it to try to block out both of these inconveniences – at least formally.

As regards the draught, this is understandable, but his dislike of the view needs a little explaining, since, with its trees (rare enough in Venice to constitute a treat), its two tiny shops (a baker's and a picture-framer's – both equally enticing, depending on your mood), a squat wellhead at its centre, and a decaying but elegant palazzo on the near side, the little clearing below is one of the loveliest spots in the whole of Venice. Joseph thinks so too, and knowing the city as well as he does he is qualified to judge. In fact, its beauty was one of the reasons why he chose these particular lodgings when first he came to Venice – that and their cheapness. Yet in spite of this it is a spot he has gradually come to dread. It is the palazzo that bothers him, you see. Not that there is anything wrong with the building itself, apart from the fact that it is a sad, lonely-looking place and has acquired a local reputation for ill luck following one or two mishaps that have taken place inside it, but because it happens to be the home of a small arch-enemy of Joseph's – one whom we have already mentioned and shall have occasion to deal with in some detail later on. It is where the Catcher lives. Or, to give him his full nickname – the one Joseph coined originally but which it now offends him to use without telescoping – it is where the Cat-fisher lives. And it is where he sits for hours on end, practising the hobby which has earned him his nickname, dangling his hook from the window in search of victims, grinning complacently in Joseph's direction and sending him slowly to distraction. Unfortunately, try as he may, there is little Joseph can do about this. He cannot intervene and put a stop to things by ordinary means, for there is the canal between him and his tormentor, and by the time he has shuffled downstairs and out into the street, crossed the bridge further down, and reached the other side, it is usually too late: the victim is hooked already, dangling high up in the air above him – out of reach and beyond his help. And he cannot intervene by professional means either, for the simple reason that in the language he does his work in there is no suitable word for him to use. (Well, strictly speaking, he could at a pinch try using a close equivalent, I suppose, such as 'little lion' or something like that, but, apart from the fact that it may not have occurred to him, I think he does not really relish the idea of exposing himself to the Catcher in this way, or of letting him witness yet another failure. For a man of his age it is shaming enough to be ranged against such a youthful enemy in the first place, without letting him see how easily he is winning.)

Once all this is understood, it is less surprising that the sight of the house opposite tends to get on Joseph's nerves, and that he spends a great deal of his valuable time nailed to the window, trying to get a glimpse of what is going on inside. What worries him especially is what happens to the cats afterwards. How does the Catcher conceal the traces of his crimes, he often wonders? Why is it that no one but himself seems to be aware of his grisly trade? And why is it that no one takes him seriously when he tries to denounce it?

Everyone he has accosted so far on the matter has just smiled at him tolerantly and replied: 'Ma sono ragazzate, Professore.' Harmless mischief. Boys will be boys. Even Trevisan to whom he once spoke most earnestly on the subject was of the same opinion. Italian children, he explained to Joseph proudly, were never really cruel. Mischievous, maybe – 'birichini', as he put it, wagging an index finger and smiling a knowing little smile – but never cruel. Perhaps his friend was a little over-tired these days. Over-worked. Cats were dying all over Venice merely because there were so many of them. The Venetians were inured to this by now. Why, only a couple of hundred years ago there had been a public sport-cum-pastime in which a cat was tied vertically to a post, and the young men would shave their heads and see who could ram it to death with the least scratches. Had Joseph never heard of this? It was a most interesting piece of folklore. No, he confirmed, stretching back in his chair and politely stifling a yawn, the Venetians never worried overly about the plight of their feline production. 'They worry', he added with still more discernible pride, 'about more important matters.'

So now Joseph has stopped mentioning it. It is, he realizes, something he must deal with on his own. Fortunately, however, things quieten down at night, especially in the winter: there are fewer cats about for one thing, and then it is term-time and the Catcher presumably has other things to do, like sleeping and doing his homework (although Joseph has recently begun to doubt that he does either). So Joseph can afford to ignore the window for this evening and get down to a quiet session of whatever it is that he does.

Giving a final twitch to the curtain, he makes first for the bathroom, where he hangs his raincoat under the shower. Next he hangs his trousers and jersey on the bulbless stumps of a chandelier over the bed, removes the bedcover and wraps himself in it for warmth. Then, after fishing out a square of pizza from his briefcase – tapping it on the table and marvelling at its unique dryness – he pulls up a chair, places an air-cushion on it, takes pen and paper and after a few preliminary shiftings and rustlings is soon deep in his task. From the narrative position adopted in this section, all we can strictly affirm is that he is reading photocopied material and doing the occasional doodle in the notebook at his elbow. His intense concentration emerges from the engrossed way in which he scratches at his head now and again with the hand that holds the pen, tracing little paths of ink across the balder patches. There is not even the title of the work to go by, it being written on the front page only and this being folded back out of sight. However, on the shelves above the table where he is working, cheek by jowl with a collection of tatty dictionaries, three translations of the Old Testament and a set of what seem to be diaries, delicately bound and initialled in gold Cyrillic letters, are some curious-looking works – fat, uneven and covered amateurishly in brown paper – the texts of which when compared with the doodlings look as if they may well have been copied out in the very same ink and by the same hand. A random selection of titles runs: *Maaseh Bereshith – Excerpts*; *Havdalah* – Rabbi Akiba; Heinrich Cornelius Agrippa ab Nettesheim – *De Occulta Philosophia*; Johannes Reuchlin (Capnion) – *De Verbo Mirifico*; J. Trithemius – *Steganographia*. One particularly bulky volume just says *Picatrix* without qualification or mention of an author.

For some learned people this list may already provide an insight, but a much more telling one could be gained at this stage if we gave up the viewpoint of an outside observer looking out, and went back to the closer although not necessarily clearer one of the outside observer looking in. This, in fact, we shall shortly do. It may also occasionally prove helpful to take up a third and yet more intimate position, that of being on the inside and looking out; or even the fourth and most intimate of all – again no intrinsic guarantee of clarity – that of being inside and looking in. And all this in order to discover not only what Joseph does, but why he does it, how he does it and, last but not least, *whether* he does it. The Signora next door is the only person so far who would answer this last query in the affirmative – and a heavily qualified one at that – and there is no compelling reason why we should take her word for it. We are unlikely to meet her, but, despite the practicality of her calling, she is, believe me, a rather fanciful woman.

III

JOSEPH thumbed through the pages before him, rigid with
impatience. It was Marsilio Ficino at his most fey, waffling
on about the finer points of astrological music – how to
capture the benign influences of the planets through an arrangement of sounds – how best to attract the spirit of each planet.
For Venus, so he maintained, you needed something 'voluptu-
ous'; 'grave' music for Jupiter; and for Apollo, the sun, something 'venerable, simple and earnest'. All very fine, thought
Joseph irritably, for a professional composer, but a tall order
for anyone who like himself had difficulty in thinking up a mel-
ody in the first place, let alone giving it a style. Ficino was an old
love of his, one of the first in fact, and one to whom he owed a lot
from the point of view of inspiration, but he was, of course, as
Joseph now felt himself competent to judge, a hopelessly subjective magician. Joseph had long since discovered that it was no use
trying to go about working magic on the self alone and hoping to
spark off from such a base a kind of home-made generator for
producing more power. Magic, to qualify as such, had to be
objective and above all operative. You had to be able to actually
see it working, and not just to feel it flowing through your
person in the form of a potential or a mere disposition. No
magician of the post-scientific age could possibly be content any
more with this kind of rambling over inward states of consciousness. Yes, with no qualms at all, he could safely lay Ficino aside.

He gathered the pages together, stacked them in their makeshift binding and stood them beside two other similar volumes

bearing the shared title *De Triplici Vita*, on the topmost shelf of his rack. There were forty or more books there already, most of which had a dusty, unopened air about them, confirming that their relegation to the upper shelf was not merely a question of place.

He scanned the shelves and blew ineffectually at the dust. This rereading was a necessary step, of that he was sure, but all the same he sometimes could not help wondering whether he was not cheating a little over all this thoroughness, and whether it did not really spring from a reluctance to close with these friends of the past or, worse still, from a reluctance to get on with the other tasks before him, rather than from a genuine fear of having missed something of importance. He knew most of the material by heart now anyway. From the position he had now reached it was easy to separate the weighty from the inessential; he could do it indeed almost with the mechanical ease of a thresher – chaff on one side, corn on the other. He smiled for a moment as he remembered what difficulty he had once had over this. The amount of time that was wasted, he thought, shaking his head ruefully as he recalled how he used to experiment to the letter with the various, far-fetched techniques which Ficino and his disciple Diacceto recommended. Natural magic be blowed. He had tried Ficino's diet, and had nibbled conscientiously on white sugar and cinnamon for hours on end. He had bought himself a saffron-yellow dressing-gown on Diacceto's suggestion, and when it had turned out to be not only useless but unbecoming as well, he had replaced it by a coal-black one – reputedly a good colour for getting on the right side of Saturn. (He wore it still as a matter of fact, but only because he couldn't afford a new one.)

During one shaming period, he even seemed to remember getting up at daybreak and chanting Pletho's hymns to the rising sun. And what had all this brought him? Nothing. Nothing at all, except a sore throat, and nagging indigestion from too much cinnamon in his food. He had spent . . . how long? – gracious, it must have been nearly five whole years – experimenting with talismans alone, without the least hint of success. A positive result in the end, he supposed, since it had enabled him to eliminate them from his arsenal for good. Five expensive, messy years they had been too, spent with paints and clay and plasticine, and constantly tacky fingertips.

Sins of youth, though, he thought tolerantly; follies of inexperience. All this, of course, had been before he had discovered the 'vis verborum' – the power of words – and before he had struck that revelational passage (in Pico's Fifteenth Magical Conclusion, if he remembered rightly) where it was plainly stated that no magical operation could ever work without cabala. This had been the great turning-point, the discovery of the Path of the Names: the long-awaited moment when he had been able to forget everything else and get down to specialization. Within the space of hours – overnight, to be precise, for it had been evening when he had begun his reading – he had become a cabalist. Not a successful one, mind you, because the breakthrough itself had come later on, but it was fair to say that since then there had been no looking back – not over essentials anyway – and he had rapidly been able to whittle down his equipment to a mere pen, a notebook, and a couple of revolving-wheels. The disappointing collection of talismans, the ludicrous robes, the herbs and the poorly composed music had been thrown respectfully but with a feeling of release into the lagoon; and with the exception of wine (which in complete accord with Ficino he still found admirable stuff for a magician when he could afford it), he had gone back to a normal diet and kept normal hours. There was no more bother about getting up at sunrise, or waiting for the zenith of the moon, since cabala besides being pocketable could be computed at any time of day. All you had to do was to know the proper names of things (although that in itself, to be honest, had taken him nearly a lifetime), work out their numbers, and then sit down to think.

He reached for his pen and began to roll up his sleeves. All these years of study and experiment would be wasted though, he told himself briskly, if he didn't manage to tie it all up, and fairly quickly. He tapped his fingers one by one on the table-top: reread – well, he could consider that accomplished; cross-examine his only potential legatee; get on with the business of writing out the testament; and . . . he looked up at the window for a moment and then quickly down again . . . ah yes, put a stop to the Catcher's little unpleasantnesses. Well *that*, at least, however upsetting to him and to the cats, was a minor matter compared to the others. It was the testament that now claimed his attention. Purposefully he drew a large bundle of papers towards him, lit a cigarette, stubbed it out reluctantly, relit it and began to write.

'Last Will and Testament of Joseph Wilhelm Kestler – Venice, November 1982', he wrote carefully in his best hand-writing, and sat for some moments looking at it. Stilted, he thought; stilted and pompous. He crossed it out and wrote in its stead: 'Findings of a Successful Twentieth-Century Magician, by J. W. Kestler'. Frivolous-sounding, he thought vexedly, and possibly a shade too fictional as well. He reached for a fresh sheet of paper and studied it hard through narrowed eyes, holding it up against the light as if confident that a suitable title would swim towards him out of the blankness – something short and clear and precise. When it did, it was so immediately satisfactory that although it came to him in Russian he let it stand. 'Zapoved', he wrote in the top left-hand corner and underlined it twice. 'Zapoved,' he whispered to himself as he did so. Zapoved. Not an original title, since it merely meant 'testament', but right somehow. Fitting. One that belonged.

And with this minor creative problem settled, the rest of the composition flowed smoothly from his pen, so long had he been carrying it around with him in sentence form inside his head. He began in large, clear letters:

I, Joseph Kestler, leave these papers in the hands of my trusted friend [here he left a blank, long enough to insert Trevisan's full title, for although the implications of 'Dottore' in Italy were virtually nil, he knew what a stickler he was for such things], confident that they will reach through his agency none but the most attentive and sympathetic reader. I write, therefore, as if addressing in the person of the future reader another close and trusted friend, whose friendship a mere discrepancy in time has prevented me from enjoying. First, a little – a relevant minimum – about myself. My interest in magic was born if not with me then at least with my awareness, for I cannot remember a time when it did not occupy me to the exclusion of all other interests. A strong psychological factor stimulating this interest may well have been – must indeed have been, else I were not fully human – the loss of my parents and family when, as a child, they were imperfectly shot and then burned in my presence; but it was neither a prime nor a causal factor. Indeed, I think I may confidently affirm that I have never studied magic for power or for revenge, but have studied it throughout from a simple desire to pursue the truth.

Here, though, he had to stop and think for a moment. For, despite the rather glib way he had just dealt with it in writing, the incident had been so very terrible and had left such a searing scar on his memory, that he wondered whether he ought not in all conscience devote a little more space to it. What he had said was perfectly true, as far as it went: it had not influenced his choice of profession on the rational plane. Not consciously. But it had branded him so deeply in other areas that he doubted he could altogether rule out the possibility of subconscious influence of some kind. He had not read his Freud in vain. How could any child who has seen his father smoulder like a log within touching distance of him remain uninfluenced by it, for goodness' sake? When he has heard him calling out for help and been unable to do anything, or even understand what he was being asked to do? Why, even now he could hardly bear to think of it: not so much the scene itself, or the smell, but the way his father had stared at him, willing him to understand whatever it was he was trying to tell him, and his own feeling of stupidity and helplessness in failing to catch his words. (Not that he had really been to blame, of course, when the words had come out in such a jumble.) If he was aiming at the truth, shouldn't he give the reader at least an insight into this more personal side of his history? Or would it merely be over-scrupulous of him – given the scientific cast of the work? Oh dear, it was a difficult question. Probably the best way out of it was just to think that if Freud himself, for example, had wasted time describing his own motives for studying the human psyche instead of getting on with the job and studying it, he would never even have got started. That was it. No digressions. They were best left to commentators later on. He resumed at a brisker pace:

Systematic study, however, did not begin until my twenty-first year, when ridding myself of the last threads of arrogance but holding fast to my presumption (how else could I have remained a magician in a world where all the finer intellects had at least temporarily deserted this profession?), I decided to examine in minutest detail the works of every distinguished magician who had preceded me. (See Appendix A for alphabetical list of authors. Those marked by an asterisk are the ones to whom I am most heavily indebted and make compulsory reading. An underlined name means that this author's works contain scattered but valuable suggestions – more detailed reference to these can be obtained from Appendix B. A name in round brackets indicates that the author can safely be ignored. Square brackets indicate authors whom it is actually wiser not to read for fear of running into confusion and contradiction. And I have used, following contemporary logicians, the swung dash or negation sign to signal those authors who must on no account be consulted for any purposes other than out-and-out refutation. Where no sign accompanies a name, the reader is left to his own devices, the omission implying that I have no feelings either one way or the other. It will be noted that these are very few.)

From a distillation of the helpful, not to say invaluable, information gleaned from my readings, I have over the years and by means of untiring experiment developed the unique and, I make bold to claim, uniquely successful method that is set out in the following pages. I intend, however, in order to establish as close contact as possible with my reader, to preface the exposition of method by a brief chronological account of my discovery, followed by an even briefer warning.

At this point, however, instead of launching into the story of the breakthrough Joseph paused again, reshuffled the order of the noun phrases in the last line and, after a short bout of coughing and puffing, headed a clean page with the subtitle 'WARNING', in bold capitals, and underlined it in three different colours of ink.

WARNING – or the importance of what Bodin calls the 'Droict Usage' of magic. Reader, friend, kindred mind, whoever you may be who take these pages in your hand and draw your eyes from line to line to decipher from their flat and finite surface the message, the technique and the powerful pragmatics that they contain, do not I beg you underestimate their danger. One of my great cabalist masters, Giovanni Pico della Mirandola, writes: 'Qui operatur in Cabala . . . si errabit in opere aut non purificatus accesserit, devorabitur ab Azazale.' This cautionary reminder, although couched in the somewhat quaint idiom of a fifteenth-century Christian believer, is one that must be taken with extreme seriousness. I do not mean, of course, as Pico so evidently does, that there is any concrete risk that an incompetent magician or one whose preparation in the discipline is incomplete will be gobbled up by the evil angel Azazael; or that in any figurative sense he will be possessed or taken over by veritable agents of evil, when the existence of such entities must surely be as insubstantial as that of dragons, mountains made of spun sugar, or even, in another and sterner key, of square triangles. Evil, by its very definition, is what I personally term an 'omissive' concept; meaning that it is conceptually ungenerated (and therefore empty) and must be thought of as acquiring what attributes it has by virtue of its position on the reverse side of Good. It is, so to speak, Good's shadow.

As he wrote the last sentence, he could not help feeling a

funny sort of itching going on somewhere in the back of his mind, as if there was some detail, presently overlooked, that was calling for his attention. He reread it carefully. Yes, he thought; although it was one he had often mulled over and was very familiar with, there was something not quite right about the shadow metaphor. Or else the metaphor itself was not at fault, but reminded him of something that was. But what? The only thing he associated with shadow himself – apart from the natural phenomenon – was the horrid little Catcher, who seemed to live under a permanent patch of it, no matter how sunny the weather. In fact, come to think of it, he could never remember seeing them out together, the Catcher and the sun. But the boy had interfered with his work enough as it was, and the matter was too insignificant to waste time on now. Enough of these interruptions. If there was anything important about it, no doubt it would come back to him later. He wrote on firmly, limiting himself to giving his head a good scratch with the pen:

I do, however, agree whole-heartedly with the negative content of Pico's reminder: namely, that no good can come either to the magician or to the world in general that contains him, unless his operative capacity is backed by a thorough understanding of what he is doing and by a sincere desire to devote his peculiar abilities to the service of that world. This entails, first and foremost, that he possess a clear, unwavering and basically correct scale of cosmic values. For the purpose of establishing the correctness of your personal scale, friendly reader and would-be disciple, I have provided in Appendix C a short but reliable ethical questionnaire to which, before reading further, you should refer. There is a straightforward method of quantifying your performance which consists in the scoring of three points for each 'a' answer, two for each 'b', and one for each 'c'. If the answer is an utterly honest 'don't know', then this may count as half a point. Whosoever totals a score of less than thirty-three points or has indulged in cheating should desist from further ambition in the field of magic.

Here he stretched out a hand automatically for his packet of cigarettes, and placing one, unlit, between his teeth, where he began to roll it rhythmically from one side of his mouth to the other, reread the last paragraph with a worried frown. He was not quite happy about the questionnaire, either. It constituted, it was true, an impediment of a sort for an already well-intentioned disciple, but it meant placing a lot of weight on Trevisan's diligent filtering. How far could he rely on this? And who, after Trevisan, would be the next custodian? And the next? And the next? What if they did not share his diligence? What if despite their care it fell, as it might so easily do in the incalculable stretch of time that might have to elapse before reaching the right ones, into the hands of an unworthy reader? Could he really expect that such a reader would be held up by this simple expedient of self-examination? It would be paradoxical if it were so. The unworthy reader would not give two fig-seeds for the questionnaire and what it stood for. Only a worthy reader with a respectable count of, say, thirty-two to thirty-five (for he had had at least the foresight to leave an ample margin) would be brought to a dismayed standstill by such a ploy, and this was not what the test was supposed to accomplish. No, he thought crossly; no, this would not do at all. His work had not cost him a lifetime of effort merely to become the facile instrument of any unscrupulous set of fingers that happened to pick it up. It must be better guarded in its journey through time, when neither he nor Trevisan would be there to watch over it and safeguard it from improper use. It must be encased and protected. It must be rendered capable of looking after itself. But how could this be accomplished save by building into the work itself a kind of safety device? Yes, a foolproof *and* scoundrelproof safety device. That was what he needed.

Well then, how about concealing some of the more vital pieces of information in the form of conundrums, he wondered, and then dotting them about the work at random so that only intelligence coupled with great tenacity would be able to unearth them? That might be a good idea, for a start. Or else what about leaving out one of the key instructions and putting in a clue instead – again in heavily riddled form – as to where to find it? Either of these ploys would be sufficient to throw an *incompetent* reader off the scent, but then incompetence was not the same thing as unworthiness. Not at all. In fact, come to think of it, they were two failings that were unlikely to be found in the same person. He could – indeed he must – guard against the first by including a few brain-teasers, but he must also think up a way of protecting his secrets against the second.

He gave his head another furious scratch with the nib. Ah well, if the worst came to the worst, he supposed he could always fall back on the classic solution (in the end he knew he'd probably have to use it anyway, willy-nilly) but it was so drastic that he didn't really like to at this stage. It would only do as a last resort, when every other alternative had been examined and found wanting. He was a magician, after all, not a murderer.

With this he sighed, glanced at his watch, tapped it severely as if to punish it for reminding him of the rapidly passing time, and began to tackle the section on the history of his discovery.

IV

S O THE truth of the matter, the answer as to what Joseph's
real profession is, and the one exceptional thing about him
that we have tried in vain so far to guess from outward
appearances, is that he is a magician. Not, it must straightway be
made clear, a conjurer, a trickster, a practitioner of legerdemain
or an illusionist of any kind, nor yet, at the opposite extreme of
gravity, a necromancer. But a learned and dignified magician. A
sorcerer, if you prefer. An enchanter. Or else, to use a word
which itself suggests a certain amount of wisdom and thus of
knowledge, a wizard.

With all the dusty disrepute which these terms have managed
to pick up over the centuries, though, causing them to crop up in
our minds accompanied by a faintly ridiculous appanage of
pointed hats, wands, brews, concoctions, spells and so forth, and
were it not for Joseph's lack of personal panache, he is perhaps
better compared to a Renaissance magus — one of those majestic
forerunners of his whose works rest on the shelf above his inky
head, faithfully copied by him by dint of Biro and the muscles of
his own hand. Better still, if this term too did not drag behind it
yet another cloud of misleading images, one could perhaps
describe him as a cabalist, although, of course, with certain
reservations. For one thing, Joseph's brand of cabalism has little
in common with that of the obscure charlatans who over the
centuries have spent their time and other people's money in
trying to obtain from words alone some tangible form of worldly
gain, and still less with that of the crouched and fasting mystics

who have confided in the disciplinary stress itself to bring its own ineffable kind of recompense. His is neither chicanery nor mysticism, but an up-to-date, practical cabalism of practically-minded and limited pretensions. That is how he thinks of himself: a scientific cabalist magus with his head screwed on, busily carrying on the uncompleted work of his great predecessors, guided by their insights and fired by their still discernible enthusiasm, the last link of a chain of minds (most, he humbly owns, much better than his own) which stretches back via the magi of the Renaissance, via the Spanish mediaeval cabalists, the Arab scholars, the Neoplatonists and Pythagoreans, to the ancient seers of Babylon and Egypt. Like his predecessors, he knows that for each single link the weight is so heavy as to be almost unbearable. There are the plodding, dull, confused days to contend with, when the load of facts and hypotheses and possible permutations lie on the researcher's brain like a cobweb spun in lead until he can feel an actual flattening and enmeshment of its tissues, and which in his own case have outnumbered the good by roughly 13,212 to 108. There are the hazards from without and the hazards from within. True, no demon has possessed him yet, to his knowledge, and in this age of relative tolerance to oddballs no one has persecuted him for his opinions, but he knows from his studies that others have not been so lucky: Pico, for example, was grilled by the Inquisition until forced to retract; Bruno was grilled by them in a more literal sense; and the poor, homeless Agrippa, his faithful black dog at his side, was hounded like a leper out of nearly every town in Europe. Mindful of these and countless others, he has calculated the risks and made his own (luckily less flamboyant) type of sacrifice.

Unlike his predecessors, however, he has the satisfaction of knowing beyond a doubt that victory is within his grasp, although this is a strong claim to put forward and needs investigating. His successes to date are, in fact, two. Number one was nothing more than a small, tentative experiment with a raindrop – flimsy enough proof in itself, maybe, since raindrops are fairly predictable in their behaviour and the choices open to them are few – but the second was a more ambitious one altogether, involving as it did no mere drop of water this time but a real, live locust, and quite a large one too. Towards the climax of the experiment, it is true, he was unfortunately interrupted, the concentration it had taken him one and a half hours to build up and over twenty years to identify was abruptly broken, and he had reluctantly to switch his gaze from the understanding in the locust's eyes to the palpable bewilderment in those of the poor Signora from next door. But all the same it was an occasion of great significance. For whereas over the raindrop he had merely proved his power in a rather subjective way, with the locust he had confirmed it. It was there to call on when wanted, to demonstrate to others under the most stringent laboratory conditions, and – with a little more skill and practice – to teach them to develop for themselves.

This, anyway, is what he felt at the time, and what he still feels about the matter. Small wonder then that, having achieved what he considers such a unique position with regard to his forerunners, he is now worried about finishing his testament, and about whom to leave it with when it is completed. The crux of the matter is this: he is the last link of the chain – well and good – but of whatever service can he be to this famous chain if, having continued it, reforged its weaker points, polished it clean, and brought it into shining and triumphant working order for the first time in history, he remains not only relatively but absolutely its last link? Understandably, though, Joseph himself doesn't like dwelling on it in such stark terms.

V

'PROFESSORE stimatissimo!' Most highly esteemed Professor! Dr Trevisan leapt to his feet with an alacrity and enthusiasm that toppled the small table where he had been sitting and sent a shower of schnapps over his pack of already untidy and sticky playing cards. Joseph watched his efforts at righting the minor disaster with forbearance. Respect of formalities was one of the mainstays of their relationship. It kept Joseph from yawning over their sometimes lengthy games, and checked any impatience that Trevisan might sometimes have felt over Joseph's tenuous grip on all things mathematical. It must therefore be observed and even fostered. He accepted a clammy handshake with a smile and returned the ornate greeting, hoping inwardly that the mishap would make the cards unusable and give him more time for the sounding-out of Trevisan. Time had become too precious to waste on cards and calculations, and, anyway, the mathematical part of his theory had turned out to be much simpler than he had thought. He was a trifle uneasy about revealing this to Trevisan, though, after all the effort and goodwill he had put into the venture. He had so shamefully overpicked the poor fellow's brains one way and another that it seemed heartless to tell him to what little effect. At one time, for example, when he had felt that the geometrical approach was going to prove a fruitful one, he had had poor Trevisan explain the rudiments of non-Euclidean geometries to him for seventeen Wednesdays running before realizing that they were getting nowhere. Another time, he had been seduced by Dee's hunches on proportion, and had insisted on their setting about number theory from the base upwards (*and* downwards come to think of it) until his friend had wilted under the strain. On all too many occasions, in fact, he had led the long-suffering doctor up blind alleys. Or rather, they had teetered up them together, the mathematician in the lead and Joseph with his scantier abilities limping along behind, making suggestions which he hoped would prove enlightening but which usually just opened up welters of yet longer and yet blinder alleys. Trevisan had never wavered and never complained. No doubts could be thrown on his reservoir of patience; that much was certain.

'Perhaps if I ordered a small carafe of water?' Trevisan suggested contritely. 'It is lucky your papers were not on the table. I'll see what I can do with a drop of water and some tissues. I may be able to clean things up.' He smiled apologetically at Joseph who smiled back. 'Although I do *feel*', he added politely, 'that we ought to lay the cards aside for this evening and do a spot more work on our figures. Last week, if I remember rightly, we were examining the possibility of applying Gödel numbering to a small class of imperatives.'

The word 'imperatives' was uttered with a sad, downward lilt, making it clear to Joseph that Trevisan too was beginning to have doubts about the usefulness of their latest scheme. So much the better, he thought relievedly, it would make his disappointment over the scant weight of the mathematical component easier for him to bear.

'Dear Dr Trevisan,' he said reassuringly, trying not to show satisfaction at the way things were turning out, 'why don't we find another table and forget about your cards *and* my papers for the present? We have spent so much time together but rarely granted ourselves the luxury of simple conversation. There are one or two things of a somewhat intimate nature that I have long been wanting to ask you. Intimate, and . . . urgent,' he added carefully. 'This is, in fact, the reason for my inviting you here this evening without waiting for our usual Wednesday meeting, and why I insist – yes *insist* – that we make it supper and that you be my guest.'

The doctor's thick eyebrows rose in surprise, lifting his spectacles with them, and he wrapped up the playing cards obediently in a large, crumpled handkerchief and looked round for a second table. 'I shall try to clean them up for next time,' he said wistfully, 'but, yes, a meal and a little conversation would be very nice indeed. Only I'd prefer it if we went halves over the bill – alla Romana. As the Romans do.'

Joseph tutted an adamant refusal. Singling out a small corner table in the most out-of-the-way recess of the crowded restaurant, he led the mathematician by the hand and settled him down in a chair with his back to the rest of the room. After a long, absorbing conversation with the waiter, and a visit to the kitchen where huge basins of fish were ranged according to their species as in a zoo, he ordered dressed crab and white wine for them both. It was years since he had allowed himself to indulge in the more expensive varieties of seafood, and he could not help feeling a twinge of regret at having left it so late. Dr Trevisan seemed satisfied with the choice and sat contemplating the wall, on which hung a series of dun-coloured oils depicting copulating beasts, with benign expectancy.

Spurred by the necessity of making a beginning, however clumsy, Joseph shifted himself firmly between his guest and the pictures and launched without preliminaries into his proposed enquiry. As a first, cautious move, he drew from his pocket one of the pages they had been working on together the previous Wednesday, the bottom corner of which was tidily hidden from view by a large square of stapled wrapping-paper, and began to prise open the staples with a toothpick. Trevisan, who had meanwhile embarked furtively on the task of cleansing his playing cards with handkerchief, water, and a touch of spittle, left his work momentarily suspended and watched with interest as the concealing patch was removed.

Still shielding the pertinent area with his hand, Joseph turned the sheet towards him. 'Here we are!' he announced with a slight but calculated air of mystery. 'This, then, is what we have been working on all this time. I have greatly appreciated your patience and the tact you have shown in never asking me more than I was able to reveal, Dr Trevisan, but I feel that the time has now definitely come . . .' He paused for a moment and watched his friend closely in case he betray signs of too strident a curiosity — inquisitiveness, of course, was a positive quality in the profession, but the disciple of a magus or even the depositary of a magus should never possess an unhealthy amount of it, to the detriment of restraint. 'The time has now come to do away with these unsightly patches and expose to you in full the true nature of my theory.'

The effect of this first probe was unfortunately somewhat marred by the arrival of their order, and Trevisan passed it all too becomingly by tucking his napkin into the collar of his shirt and addressing the brunt of his attention to a meticulous dismemberment of his crab. Joseph decided to use more stringent tactics. He lifted his hand rapidly, placed the menu firmly over the sheet of paper and, ignoring the plate set before him, bent earnestly towards the Italian and asked quietly but with marked seriousness:

'Do you believe, Dr Trevisan, in the existence of God?'

An expression of vague alarm flickered over the doctor's face for a second before politeness could erase it. 'God?' he enquired puzzledly. 'Did you say God, caro Professore? We are getting on to intimate topics indeed this evening.' He broke a bread-stick and tapped it in fast, staccato rhythm against the rim of his glass. 'All Italians are superstitious,' he replied after a moment's reflection, 'and I am no exception. But . . . no, I wouldn't go so far as to say that I believe in God. It is not', he went on a shade more stiffly, 'a subject I have ever devoted much thought to – not, that is, since I left school. I have always been of the opinion that religion is for children really. Or for the very old. Of course, there is no telling but that I may take it up again some day.' He seemed a little dissatisfied, either by the question or by his own answer, gave a brief snort of laughter, and went back to his crab with camouflaging vigour. 'Very delicious,' he said on a happier note. 'Squisito!' and he motioned to Joseph to eat his own portion.

Joseph, however, had other things on his mind. He was not at all pleased by Trevisan's reaction to his question. If not flippantly, he had none the less responded with a certain amount of levity in dismissing religion out of hand as a brain-sop for the intellectually immature. This was not a good sign at all. He placed his hand firmly over Trevisan's to prevent the fork from reaching his mouth and fired at him, this time with unmistakable seriousness – with severity even: 'What about morality, though? What about the individual conscience? Do you believe that *that* exists, my dear Trevisan? Or is it just another trifling little question you are storing up for your dotage? A great deal hangs on your reply,' he added earnestly, gazing hard at the lowered face of his friend which had now, he noted in disappointment, taken on an expression stronger than embarrassment and only slightly weaker than fright. It put him in mind of the surgeon when he had mentioned to him the matter of his death. Was it perhaps, he wondered, a characteristic of the professional classes in Italy to fight shy of the greater issues and to give themselves over to panic when the conversation took a metaphysical turn? For panicking was what Trevisan was now doing.

'Professor' Giuseppe!' he protested feebly, flushed in the face behind his sallowness and trying to regain control of his hand. 'Professor' Giuseppe! You must realize that when a Venetian is eating a crab like this – a real, fresh granseola like this – he does not like to discuss serious things lightly . . . or light things seriously, come to that. He likes to discuss serious things seriously, and to talk only about the food. Why not try a little yourself and tell me what you think of it? This is a wonderful time of year for shellfish, you know. It is when the little crabs begin to shed their carapaces and you can eat them whole, fried in batter and parmesan. Or perhaps,' he went on lyrically, his embarrassment outweighed by the interest of the subject, 'perhaps you *feed* them on batter first and then fry them, so that the egg is on the *inside*. Yes, that's the way it is. You keep them in a dish of beaten egg until they have eaten it all up – they are very greedy little animals, you see – and then you pop them into a pan of boiling oil. Le moleche, they are called. Did you ever try them?'

Joseph eyed his friend morosely and released his hand. Events seemed to have catapulted him from the uncomfortable position where choice of some kind had become a necessity, to the yet more uncomfortable position where it had become impossible. He was distinctly worried about Trevisan now, and was beginning to have serious doubts that, for all his goodwill and honesty, he would ever make an ideal depositary; and yet, in the minute circle of Joseph's acquaintances, he was the one and only person who could ever be seriously looked on as a candidate for this post. With these crippling premises there was little Joseph could do now except set aside his misgivings as if he had never felt them, and go ahead with the enquiry.

Dismissing the topic of fried crab with a brusqueness that seemed to unsettle Trevisan even more, he announced loudly: 'Dr Trevisan. There is another thing I have been meaning to ask you for a long time. What would you do if you came across a Rembrandt in the attic of some destitute relation of yours?'

'A Rembrandt? Destitute relations?' Trevisan looked up sharply. 'I don't think I have any destitute relations,' he said in a hurt tone of voice. 'Mine is quite a well-to-do family on the whole. Not rich, but well-to-do. A Rembrandt, too. That would be most unusual in Italy, don't you think?'

'Not necessarily a Rembrandt, then,' explained Joseph more patiently. 'What I meant was, what would your reaction be if you happened to find, let us say, an overlooked treasure – a work of art – in the possession of a poor relative of yours? If you had a poor relative, that is. As an hypothesis.'

'Ah.' The Italian's face cleared. 'Ah, an hypothesis. It is a game, I see. What would I do *if*. I see. What would my reaction be? Cosa farei? Beh . . .' He considered the matter thoughtfully as he chased the remaining fragments of crab round his plate with a crust of bread.

Joseph watched him warily. Although it seemed in a way unnecessary to spring a question like this on his friend, and naive to imagine that an answer could tell him any more than he already knew of him through years of acquaintance, he happened to set great store by the efficacy of this particular test. He had thought the matter over carefully, and had gone to considerable trouble before framing the deceptively simple question which enshrined it. Integrity – so his reasoning had gone – was a difficult virtue to simulate. Even hypothetical integrity. *Especially* hypothetical integrity. Integrity was more than a virtue, and more than a complex of virtues. It was a way of looking at things. In fact, it was a quality so deeply ingrained and pervasive as to set a kind of framework or boundary to the imaginings; and (although the converse was a trifle more doubtful) if you were incapable of imagining dishonestly, then you were incapable of acting so. This was, however, the first time he had used the test on anyone with hopes of their passing. He held his breath in suspense, and waited for the answer as to where Trevisan's boundaries lay. It was not long in coming.

'Delight,' Trevisan said simply, licking his fingers and leaning back from the table with a sigh. 'I should be delighted. Who would not?' Joseph said nothing, but went on watching with increasing wariness.

'Delighted for my relation, of course, in the first place,' Trevisan went on unconcernedly, 'but delighted for myself as well, because in a case like that I think that my hypothetical cousin or what-have-you would be bound to show his gratitude to me, the finder, as well, don't you agree? Ours is a very close-knit family,' he added smilingly, pleased at having grasped the spirit of the game.

Joseph breathed once more and looked at his friend with approval. He need not have worried; whatever his shortcomings as regards ethical theory, in actual practice Trevisan was, of course, as upright a man as it had ever been his fortunate to meet. He began to slide away the menu to show him the underlying papers, but then, thinking better of it, slid it back into place again and asked, still a little warily:

'What, if I may make so bold as to ask, what exactly do you think that my *true* purpose has been all this time? Why, apart from the mutual pleasure we obtain from our regular meetings, apart from our card games and from our – what shall I call them? – our little coaching sessions in mathematics, do you think I have trespassed on your time and patience all these years?' He stared earnestly at the long, brown face across the table.

'This is still part of the game?' the Italian enquired hopefully. Joseph shook his head. 'Well, in that case,' Trevisan replied, twiddling at the glass set in front of him and spilling more drops of liquid, 'in that case, I can only say that it isn't something I have really allowed myself to dwell on. I was sure you had your reasons.'

'Oh come, come now,' Joseph chided him. 'Tonight is a night for revelations. Let us try to forget for a moment that we have known each other so long and have got so set in our ways. I'm half afraid that our behaviour together has grown into too rigid a code. Let's try to forget the code for just a little moment and speak our minds instead.'

His friend smiled an unhappy smile: 'Very well,' he agreed dubiously, 'but it will not do to go and spoil our Wednesdays.'

Joseph found this rather touching on Trevisan's part, having himself been rather bored by their weekly meetings of late, and wondered briefly whether he should warn him how few they were likely to have ahead of them, and why this was to be so, but thought it would be too melancholy a task.

'Our Wednesdays are a source of great pleasure to me as well, Dr Trevisan,' he said quietly instead, 'and I hope we will have many more of them. But today is not a Wednesday – it is a day set apart. A conversation day for us, as I explained earlier. So why all this reticence? You would hardly have borne with me all this time if you had thought you were dealing with a crank, now would you, or with a pernicious time-waster; just because I happen to be good at playing cards?'

Trevisan drew a breath in pained surprise: 'Professor Giuseppe! Professore caro! I have, I must admit, often asked myself why you needed my help over your work, or should I say your hobby,' – Joseph flinched imperceptibly at the word 'hobby' – 'but I have always told myself, *and* my wife too when she

47

questioned me about it, that it was no business of mine. If I must be frank, then I shall tell you that the explanation lies, I think, in the fact that you are a dilettante scholar – a *deeply* committed dilettante scholar, of course – and that your particular interest lies in the Jewish mystical technique of cabala. That is all there is to it, I think: you are interested in cabala. And it is', he added, nodding his head in grave agreement, 'a very interesting field of research indeed. Very, very interesting.'

Joseph's face brightened and he set about the food before him with relish, having left it untouched so far from sheer tension. 'You are right, of course,' he confirmed between mouthfuls, 'you are right all along the line, Dr Trevisan. And I thought I had managed to conceal it from you. How foolish of me, and how unnecessary. Yes, I am very interested in cabala. I am very interested indeed. Cabala is, you might say, my reason for living.'

He was much happier about the way his friend was responding to this part of the enquiry. No surprise, no scepticism, no disapproval; and he had known about it all along. Well, well, well, he thought more comfortably, now here was a good moment to reveal himself a little further. For there was, of course, a very big difference – a gulf, in fact – between the study of cabala and the practice of it; and having got so far it would not do to leave Trevisan under any shadow of doubt on this point. Taking courage in both hands and gazing squarely into the Italian's bespectacled face (regrettably, he could not see his eyes but only two glassy miniatures of his own person – taut, tiny, and hunched with the effort of disclosure), he whispered confidentially: 'Dr Trevisan, I *am* a cabalist.'

From across the table his companion gave a pleased laugh. 'I am sure you are, by now,' he said lightly, whipping out the pack of cards from his pocket once more and going back to the polishing of them, as if to signal that there was no further call for concealment on either side. 'That's how all real scholars become in the end – immersed in their research to the point of identification. I am sure it would take me that way too if ever I went into the thing properly.'

Joseph sat back and relaxed for the first time that evening. Yes, things were going very nicely indeed. He had expected Trevisan to boggle over this point, to hold back, to express incredulity; but here he was, showing not only tolerance but also sympathetic understanding. Had he really and truly grasped the meaning of his explanation, though, Joseph wondered? Was he really aware of the difference between scholarly research on cabala on the one side and, on the other, the actual putting into practice of the discipline?

He studied the kind, attentive tilt of his friend's head with the two mirroring rectangles that hid the eyes, and put out a still bolder feeler: 'I am a *practical* cabalist, you must realize,' he said quietly, laying on the adjective all the stress he could give it and waiting breathlessly for an answer. Trevisan put aside the ace that he had been rubbing and murmured calmly: 'Quite, quite. I am sure you are. That's the way to be: practical. I suppose in a way I am a practical mathematician too. There is not much theory left in car insurance, alas.'

Joseph beamed at his friend, reached across the table and took his hand in a warm, thankful squeeze. 'Ah!' he sighed, 'that was just what I had hoped you would say. Just what I had hoped. My *very* dear Trevisan, the time has now come to let you into the heart of the mystery. Although mystery it is not at all, as you will now see for yourself.'

And so saying, he raised the menu, not without a certain flourish, to reveal the hidden script: a mass of small triangles pointing in various directions, some clustered together, some side by side, some perched uneasily one on top of the other. Trevisan eyed them appreciatively. 'And to think, Professor Giuseppe,' he said, showing what seemed to Joseph just the right amount of surprise, 'all this time I was convinced it was Hebrew you were working on. Now this,' he picked up the page and held it at arm's length, squinting over the rim of his glasses, 'this, if you don't mind my saying so, doesn't look at all like Hebrew to me. Not at all. How very strange. In fact, it doesn't look to me like any language I know of. It *is* a language, I suppose?'

Joseph nodded. He had been savouring this moment ever since

he had first thought of letting Trevisan in on the secret. 'It is indeed,' he said proudly. 'It is one of the oldest, if not *the* oldest alphabet in the world – or so modern scholarship would have us believe. It is', he took a deep breath and a sip of his wine, and whispered reverentially, 'Ugaritic. The language of cabala.'

'Ugaritic. Interesting,' said Trevisan, 'I never realized the cabalists used Ugaritic. I thought that, their being Jews, they must have used Hebrew. Not that I have ever given a great deal of thought to the matter, of course. Now this *is* interesting.' He swivelled round on his chair to keep a check on the diminishing activity in the restaurant, and took a stealthy peep at his wrist-watch.

Joseph stretched out an arm and swivelled him gently into place again. 'As regards the mediaeval cabalists you are right, of course,' he said solemnly. 'How could they, when it was to them a lost language?'

The doctor responded with a suitably impressed nod. 'How indeed?' he agreed diffidently. 'How indeed?'

'The original cabalists, on the other hand – the pioneers, let us call them,' went on Joseph, enchanted to have an audience at last – and such a satisfactory one too, 'now they were a different matter. The language was there for them to make use of, and I have compelling reasons, dear Dr Trevisan, to think that make use of it they did.' He paused to let his words make due effect.

Trevisan fingered a grubby king and wiped it delicately on both sides. 'I feel my wife would make a better job of it than I,' he sighed, placing the card on top of the small pile he had already treated, where it stuck like a magnet. 'I have never yet come across a stain that was able to fox her, although I seem to remember her running into bad trouble with some blackberries once.' The memory seemed to afford him private and faintly malicious amusement but, noticing the urgency in Joseph's face, he checked himself, blended his laugh into a cough and added hastily: 'So they used this Ugaritic then, did they? Very, very interesting indeed. You must tell me all about it one of these days in detail when you have time. It will add spice to our little sessions. I see now your reason for all the secrecy: you feel that this will come as something of a bombshell to the academic world. You could have trusted me though, you know. You *ought* to have trusted me. I know how envious these professional scholars can be, especially when the discovery comes from someone like yourself who is not part of their tight little world.' This aspect was one that he seemed to find more stimulating. 'Mafiosi!' he added loudly, causing a few heads to turn in their direction. 'Mafiosi, that's what they are, the lot of them. Many years ago now I was offered a job at the University myself, you know, but I turned it down, and never regretted it. I didn't want to get drawn into those circles. Mafia. Mafia.' He righted his glasses, which had come somewhat awry as he had been speaking: 'When are you thinking of publishing your results?'

Joseph, who with a see-sawing of his impressions had found these last remarks rather worrying, ignored the question and instead asked anxiously: 'You have a few contacts still, though, at the University here?'

'Oh yes indeed,' replied Trevisan, coughing modestly to mask his evident pride. 'I am not as out of touch as all that. I don't mingle with academics for choice, but yes, I still have my contacts there.' He shook a reprimanding finger at Joseph, his face relaxing into an expression of conspiratorial understanding, as if he had been given sudden and welcome enlightenment on all that had been said thus far. 'Aha, Professore! *Now* I know what you are after. You would like me to perform a little introduction for you, is that it? Get people interested in your work and so forth? You should have told me so straight away.'

'Yes,' Joseph admitted simply. 'Yes, that was partly what I wanted. I should like to meet one or two people there, you see, to whom I could illustrate my theories, with a view to leaving my work to the University itself one day — if this does not seem too presumptuous. The right sort of people, if you see what I mean.'

'Pah!' said Trevisan airily, dipping his fingers into the water jug and scanning the list of desserts on the menu, 'I am sure that can be arranged . . . By the way, I am told the ices here are *excellent* . . . Yes, I am sure that that could be arranged for you, caro Professore. There was no need for you, though, to make such a delicate approach; it is a little service I shall positively enjoy performing.'

Joseph thanked him. 'Of course the *completed* report of my findings won't be ready for a few weeks yet,' he added apologetically. 'I am still working on the instructions and recommendations, and there is a short chronological account of my methods of discovery to be dealt with; but in the meantime I could write them a summary, and perhaps give a small practical demonstration in order to arouse their interest.'

'Yes,' said Trevisan automatically, doing his best to catch the eye of a waiter, 'yes that would do very well. I cannot promise the attendance of the Rector himself or any bigwigs like that, you understand, but I think I can reach an associate Professor of Semitic languages and maybe a colleague or two of mine – mathematicians, of course, and not strictly connected to your field of research, but definitely the right sort of people. Would that do for a start?'

Joseph nodded gratefully. 'I shall have to procure a locust, too,' he murmured with a trace of anxiety still in his voice.

'Hmm, yes, of course,' agreed Trevisan, ordering a zabaione ice and coffee for himself. 'Are you keeping me company?'

'Just coffee, thank you,' said Joseph. 'It might be a little difficult in this season,' he added pensively.

Trevisan, his attention claimed wholly by the question of ices, demurred with a clicking noise: 'Tch, tch. On the contrary, winter is the best time for them, I always maintain.'

Joseph, however, was so grateful that he had no heart to set him right about this minor matter, or to refuse his friend's pointed invitation when, having downed zabaione, coffee and a third schnapps, he placed the deck of cards in the middle of the cloth and pronounced it in working order. What, after all, he reminded himself soothingly as he prised open with difficulty the hand he had been dealt, was the sacrifice of an hour or so of his time when in exchange he could look forward to a safe and dignified resting-place for his testament?

VI

Having had the presence of mind to lose three games to Trevisan in quick succession, Joseph got back from the restaurant quite early. And as soon as he got back he sat down to work. His earlier tiredness had left him, and not even the long walk home through the empty streets, nor the unpleasant feeling of being followed during the last stretch of it, had managed to spoil his concentration or damp his spirits.

To be quite honest, of course, they *had* been a little dampened by his friend's reaction to the first part of the enquiry. (You would have thought, he muttered to himself a shade bitterly as he tested his air-cushion for buoyancy and sat himself gingerly down on it, that a mathematician, of all people, would have a better grasp of fundamentals. God, religion, belief, all brushed lightly aside in favour of a plate of dressed crab – that had upset him deeply.) But on the whole he was satisfied with the way things had gone. Trevisan surely would never have agreed to arrange a meeting with members of the University if he had not thought the theory worthwhile. It was not going to be easy, though, to prepare the summary that he had promised to have ready on the day, seeing that his work was already the distillation of a lifetime's study, and hardly susceptible, therefore, to any more squeezing. He would have to omit a lot. A pity, but there it was. No use in burdening them with too much material; it would only put them off. On the other hand, to make it at all complete – not to mention comprehensible – he would have to include a little bit about the use of names, and a little bit too on

53

the 'Urwert', or original values of letters, from which, and from which alone, the names derived their power. He could probably leave the history of operative magic safely aside without muddling his audience too much, and could skate lightly over the techniques of the earlier and less successful cabalists; but he most certainly couldn't afford to understate his case as regards the actual breakthrough. Should he, he wondered, mention the golem too while he was about it? It would probably be a rather daring move, especially if the other mathematicians turned out to be as blithely agnostic as their colleague, but it did after all represent the turning-point of his whole career. It had been the moment of sudden insight, when he had felt (as Archimedes and Newton were reported to have felt, but probably never did, it being so trite) an actual beam make its way through the skull and cortex and burst into a great flash of light inside. Yes, he would have to include a brief report on the golem episode and the clue that it had given him; but how was he going to fit it all in?

He drew his scattered papers wearily before him and tried, as he had enviously watched the surgeon doing, to tidy them up a bit. As he did so, tussling with them and catching at the odd sheet as it fluttered to the floor, he could not help wondering for a moment how his inside was coping in this respect. Were things still tolerably tidy and functional there, he asked himself anxiously? Were all the pieces still intact? He doubted they were. Come to think of it, he could feel at this very moment a nasty, stabbing pain in his left side. Could it be due to the crab? Perhaps it had been unwise of him to order it. Or perhaps the crab was not to blame, and it was simply that his general condition was indeed worsening. If so, then there was no time to lose; he must ignore the pain and set to work immediately.

He pushed back his sleeves and chewed thoughtfully at the cap of his pen. Well, to start with, he had better deal with his spoken address to the audience, and leave the summary until later, when he had decided which points needed more than oral coverage. Like that, he would be loosened up before he got to the difficult part. It might be a good, attention-claiming move to begin with a quotation. He wrote painstakingly:

From the Ugaritic cycle of the deeds of Keret, King of Khubur, circa 1800 B.C. (Own translation.) 'Then the clement and merciful El said: Be reseated, my sons, on your princely thrones. For I will work a creation: I will create a female creature who will vanquish the evil, who will banish the disease.' So saying, he filled his hand with clay, his right hand with the purest clay, and hardened it to stone . . .

This, to his knowledge, was the first account ever recorded of golem-making and – popular or not – he thought it could hardly fail to make them sit up. Interesting too that the original golem had been a female, he thought fleetingly; he had never really dwelt on the possible implications of this, but there was no time to do so now. He must get on with the address.

Signori, from the moment my eyes rested on the words of this ancient and beautiful poem, that had lain buried for centuries beneath . . .

No, no, no. This would not do at all. He must try to be as brief and to the point as possible. He crossed out the offending lines and began afresh:

Signore e Signori [which made a better opening, for there might well be lady mathematicians present], when by fortunate chance these words came to my notice, I immediately realized their significance as regards my own theories on practical cabala.

There, that sounded better. Insufficiently dramatic, maybe, but more controlled and informative. Of course (although it would never do to tell them anything of the kind), in actual fact it had been a moment of high drama: a rapturous, once-in-a-lifetime experience which he would never forget.

He leant back dreamily in his chair, gazing at the pattern of cracks and damp on the wall above, and allowed himself a short, nostalgic pause. He had been sitting right here, in this very

55

chair, when it had happened, reading an article which he had come across in some German periodical or other that he had picked up at the library – an article on the decipherment of Ugaritic nearly fifty years earlier by . . . what were the fellows' names? Surely his memory would not start letting him down over a thing like this? Oh dear, why was it he had never paid more attention to Giulio Camillo's memory theatre? If only he had, there might now have been a tidy, well-stocked cupboard of information inside his head, with shelves and doors and labels, in which there would have been no need to rummage like this to find things . . . Ah, yes, by a certain Virolleaud, and Dhorme, and Bauer. Or perhaps it was Bayer. No matter. He would always be grateful to them, whatever their names were.

There had been a long and quite amusing discussion of Canaanite civilization, and then a defence of its much-maligned religious practices. The author seemed to think that the horror stories of debauchery, ritual prostitution in the temples, child-sacrifice, and so forth, had been deliberately put about by the Jewish leaders in order to win their people back from the colourful Canaanite cults to the rather drier one which they themselves championed (which couldn't have been easy for them, come to think of it, when all they had to offer was just one God whom nobody could see).

He had found this part very convincing. He had often suspected the Old Testament of partisanship – the Book of Judges in particular – and had always taken its rantings against the poor Canaanites with a pinch of salt. And here was a learned scholar of paleo-Semitic languages agreeing with him. He had read on, becoming more and more interested; but it was not until he reached a page on which there was a translation of three tablets of cuneiform script and he had learnt how the god El had made his golem Shaataqat out of clay, that the realization had hit him with full force. When it did so, suddenly, smoothly, and beauti-fully neatly, all the pieces of information which he had been storing in his mind for so long – the secret doctrines of the early cabalists; the myth of numbers; the power of names; the original language in which such names must be calculated in order to unleash their magical power; the Jews' 'idolatry' of the Canaanite deities; the Ugaritic alphabet itself with its thirty letters (exactly thirty letters: three times ten, which fitted the theory so much better than the twenty-two characters of Hebrew – hardly a coincidence, surely?) – these pieces of material that had been stored separately in little, watertight compartments of his brain, came miraculously together to form one coherent, interlocking whole. Short-sighted fool that he was, he had scolded himself excitedly, how could he have failed to understand: it was the *Canaanites*, not the Jews, who had first practised the magical art of golem-making; they had done it by using their own Ugaritic language, and the early Jewish cabalists had learnt this technique from them and had practised it also, in utmost secrecy. It was as clear and as simple as that. The conclusion too was staring him in the face: the language of cabala was not Hebrew at all, but a much older Semitic tongue – Canaanite or, to be exact, Ugaritic. Naturally, with the passage of time, either through giving way to the pressures of orthodoxy, or else from sheer forgetfulness, the secret had been lost somewhere along the way and later cabalists had gone back to Hebrew again. This was the reason why none of them had ever quite been able to recover the lost power; not even in the golden period of the Renaissance when the great brains of the Christian cabalists had set themselves to the problem and had done so much valuable work in the field. They had been barking up the wrong linguistic tree, the lot of them – or up the wrong branch, anyway. So much so that Agrippa, for example, had virtually lost patience with Hebrew altogether and had declared that any old language whatever would do for cabalistic purposes. And now here was he, plain Joseph Kestler, the last and humblest link, the lone, displaced cabalist of the twentieth century, with the problem suddenly solved.

The memory of his feelings was still strong enough to send a shiver down Joseph's spine. What a moment it had been. Yes, he must certainly let his audience share a little of that excitement. He picked up his pen and went dutifully back to his work, not pausing again until it had reached near completion; not even when a soft spate of thuds against the window made him give a violent jump and sent his pen skidding across the page in a loop. It was the Catcher up to his tricks again, he muttered to himself grimly, keeping his attention firmly on the page before him and trying to erase the loop; he was throwing stones most likely, and rattling the window-pane in order to rattle his, Joseph's, nerves. Well, he wouldn't let himself get rattled this time. His problems must be kept in strict order of precedence if all or any of them were to be solved, and the Catcher was the last on the list.

It was the more urgent problem of the address that must be tackled this evening. How much, for example, could he expect his audience to know about cabalism? Should he mention Rabbi Nahman of Brazlav? Or Isaac the Blind, or Abulafia? Would they know the difference between kabbalah and cabala? Between a form of religious mysticism on the one hand, and the channelling of certain of its techniques for magical purposes on the other? Would they be at home with the works of Reuchlin? If he quoted Agrippa's simple but basic theories on gematria, would they know what he was talking about? And how about notakarion and temurah? Might it not add a dash of prestige to his own theory if he mentioned some, or any, of his famous predecessors, Jewish or Gentile as may be, or would it merely tend to confuse? These were hard decisions to make. Perhaps he should first touch on Heinrich Cornelius Agrippa in the address, and then expand on his gematria in the written summary, and leave Reuchlin out of the picture altogether.

Deaf to a second series of thuds, he went busily on with the process of selection and his hand sped resolutely across page after page. As he neared the end, he was so pleased with what he had written that he even began to hum a little under his breath. It would be nice, he decided, fitting and nice, to end up with an open tribute to his friend. Not only would it be bound to please Trevisan personally, but it might also – who could tell – lend him a little lustre in those academic circles which, in spite of the careless way he spoke of them, he seemed still to hold in a certain awe. Something along these lines, perhaps: 'Once I had accomplished my great discovery, the person who helped me over the remaining details . . .' No, that did not sound very generous. Maybe this would be better:

Once I had hit upon my fundamental insight there remained to be settled the question of the gematria, or calculation of the numeric value of each letter of the Ugaritic alphabet. In this task I was fortunate to be able to rely on the invaluable aid of my good friend, Dr Augusto Trevisan, to whom a substantial part of my ensuing success is due.

Yes, that was better. Very neat, in fact, thought Joseph contentedly. It struck exactly the right note.

He heaved a deep sigh of relief, stacked the pages together as neatly as he could, weighted them down with an apple, and went over to the window. He opened it wide and took a deep breath of the salt-ridden air. The little square rested under a crystal stillness. The shops and houses were shuttered, but he could still make out the harmony of their shapes, and could trace the pale, marble surround of ogival arches and the curious, splayed chimney-stacks, pointing like trumpets to the sky above. Over the buildings, the trees, picked out by the light of his own window, cast their branches like a protective grille of whitish gold. He looked down on them fondly, thinking, as he so often did, that had it not been for the palazzo and the dark blotch of the Catcher's window (why, even by this light he could see the grimy, black ring round it as if someone had inked it in or smudged it with soot), then this indeed would have been the most beautiful spot in the world.

Cautiously, lest he disturb the quiet of it all, he made to close the shutters. But as his hand groped along the surface of the sill it came across a soft, damp object lying there precariously on the very edge. He picked it up and examined it, and his sense of peace and contentment left him immediately; it was – of all unwelcome objects to find resting on your window-ledge in the dead of night – a cat's paw. Recently amputated, too, by the looks of it. Joseph bowed his head in bitter recognition of the enemy's flair: while he had been busy over his work, the Catcher had not been throwing stones to distract him. Nothing so bland. He had been throwing paws.

How many paws, too, he wondered, as he held the sorry little trophy to the light to examine it closer. How many other paws had he had to throw before landing one successfully on the ledge? And how many more cats had been cut up and slain in the process? It hardly bore thinking of – yet think of it he supposed he must. Not only think of it, either. No. He must act on it. With this last atrocity, problem number four had moved up on the list and begun to call for priority treatment.

He braced his shoulders and stared hard at the window. Well then, so be it: if the Catcher wanted war, war he would get. The very next morning he would pay a visit to the parents and see if he couldn't put a stop to things that way. It was not how Agrippa and company would have tackled an enemy of ten or eleven or thereabouts (if they had ever let themselves be drawn into conflict with one so young in the first place, that is, which he doubted), but it was the strongest method he himself was willing to use at this stage.

To seal his decision he dropped the paw into the canal below, saluting it with a solemn wave of the hand, and listened for the definitive plop which would mark its arrival amongst the flotsam. A gesture he regretted immediately. For apart from the fact that the plop was followed by an unmistakable snigger from across the way (meaning that the Catcher had found this part of the proceedings particularly amusing), he realized that he should have kept the paw as evidence to support his case. Snapping his fingers crossly, he peered down at the inscrutable oily surface of the water. Never mind, perhaps at high tide he would be able to fish it out again. Yes, that was what he must do: retrieve it at high tide tomorrow and take it directly to the boy's father – or else to the police, if need be – and lodge a formal complaint.

VII

T HE VISIT to the Catcher's stronghold went off quite differently from the way Joseph had hoped it would – or even from the way he had feared. It was the first time he had ever seriously tried to close in on the enemy, and despite the exasperation which urged him onwards, he did so now with extreme reluctance. Afterwards, of course, he realized that his fears had been groundless, for it had, in fact, brought him no nearer to the child than before (if anything, quite the reverse), but he could not help feeling that it was somehow wrong for him to set foot inside the house. It smacked of defeat, and it smacked of contagion. It was raining again, lightly, when he left the pensione. He had seen the Catcher in person ten minutes earlier, setting off across the square with the usual trail of schoolfellows tagging along behind, and had waited for what he had judged a safe interval before setting forth himself and retrieving the paw from the canal.

The palazzo, he took melancholy note on entering, must once have seen brighter days. The rooms on the ground floor were high and spacious; the ceiling, upheld by slender, soaring columns of pink marble, wore its patches of damp and its peeling plaster in a graceful kind of way, a skeletal form of decoration still visible under the blemishes. A central pool of water and a painted stump of wood fringed with a brilliant ring of green showed that it had once boasted a private gondola-mooring, from the side of which a flight of wide, shallow steps, designed for the safe ascent of high-heeled slippers and sweeping skirts, led gently to the drier upper quarters. He mounted them with difficulty, stopping every third step or so to get his breath back and inhaling as he did so a mixture of smells: mould, sea-water, rancid oil and some other strange ingredient which he was irrationally tempted to identify as the stench of frightened animals.

On the first landing, as if washed up there by a freak tide, lay a collapsed rubber dinghy, and on the second rusted the wreck of a wheeled shopping basket from the top of which protruded the wing of a very dead and very dirty seagull (perhaps responsible for the fourth smell). Familiarity with the outside of the building had prepared Joseph for no such profundity of squalor. Formerly he had been shocked, if anything, by the state of abandon into which it had fallen, and by the loneliness of its stand. It had upset him to see it, like many other buildings of its kind in Venice, so uncared-for and so sparsely lived in. But now on the contrary he was shocked that it be inhabited at all, and even found himself close to making allowances for a child who had had to grow up in such an environment. It was cold too, he noticed, and the dampness bit into his throat like smoke.

Judging by the names pinned outside each door with a makeshift system of card and drawing-pin in place of the customary brass plaque, and which the damp had reduced to limp little grey flags, there seemed to be three families dwelling there in all. The apartment he was searching for was not hard to find. Its paper banner was unreadable, but no sooner had Joseph set about examining it than the door was opened to him, before he had even pressed the door-bell, as if his arrival had been expected.

In the doorway stood a young, defenceless-looking woman wearing a pair of faded jeans and carrying a very small baby, its back wedged neatly into the accommodating cavity of a colander. 'Prego?' the woman said kindly, beckoning him inside. 'You're from the pensione opposite, aren't you? I used to work there once, before I got married that is, but I don't expect you remember. You were the one with all the books.' She smiled and swirled the colander round teasingly before depositing it and its also smiling burden on the table.

The apartment, in contrast to the rest of the house, was clean and warm, the walls freshly painted and hung with colourful posters – prominent among them, Joseph noted wryly, one of a litter of kittens playing with a skein of wool. The furniture was of pale blond wood and looked as if it had been unprofessionally but lovingly constructed. Flowered cushions lay scattered over an immaculately washed floor. On a low dresser made from crates and lacquered in bright orange varnish stood a photograph of a sprucely uniformed young man, and placed centrally before it an eggcup containing a single plastic rose.

'It's about Giuseppe that you've come, isn't it?' said the young woman, shaking back the fringe of hair which shrouded her eyes and puffing at it with a faint sigh. 'I thought as much. Please sit down, and then you can tell me all about it. Would you like me to make you a cup of coffee?'

Joseph shook his head perplexedly and remaining standing. He was taken aback by this reception. In the first place, the Catcher shared his name. In the second, he had expected . . . well, what had he expected? A surly, out-of-work father, maybe; a mean-faced slut of a mother; debasing poverty, dirt, filth, overcrowding, squalling children – something of the kind. Or else gloom and petit-bourgeois rectitude, and a couple of elderly parents with faces as sour and pinched as their off-spring's. Instead of which he was confronted by this nice young girl he had once known, with a clean and well-tended baby of perfectly ordinary appearance (verging, if anything, towards the jolly), living in clean and well-tended surroundings. It did not fit in at all with the rest of the palazzo, nor with the picture he had formed of the Catcher's family entourage. It was hard to imagine him importing his sinister pool of darkness into an atmosphere like this, or his having developed it here; and hard to see him carrying out his complicated acts of cruelty without being noticed. In fact, it was hard to think of him as belonging here at all.

He played for a little more time. 'Y . . . yes,' he admitted cautiously, 'yes, it is about your son,' (he could not bring himself to use the Christian name) 'but it is a matter that I had perhaps better speak to your husband about; without worrying you personally, I mean.'

'Oh, worry!' she scoffed lightly, 'that's not a new one on me.

My husband . . .' her voice faltered as she pointed to the photograph, 'well, you see, my husband was killed just two months ago today, so it will have to be me that you tell. There's only me left.' The fringe fell back into place and she made no effort to shift it but, lifting a hand to ward off any expression of sympathy on Joseph's part, added gruffly: 'His own fault. It was a car crash. Funny, when you'd think that living here, that would be the least of your dangers.' Her voice faltered again and she looked towards the window and added slowly: 'You know, people said it was an unlucky house, this, when we moved in. But I never really listened to them. People say such a lot of things, don't they, and most of them silly.'

Then she shrugged, summoned a smile, and clasped the colander close to her again. 'Anyway, I've got this one and I've got my Giusi, so I suppose I oughtn't to complain really. What's he been up to, then? Nothing naughty, I hope? Nothing wicked? He gets on very well at school, you know, but he does land himself in scrapes sometimes. It's his high spirits. He's the *image* of his father.' And she gave Joseph a frank smile expressing tenderness and concern, but untouched by any serious trace of doubt.

Joseph coughed uneasily. He had been doing some very rapid thinking. Even assuming that he was right about the Catcher, that he was not himself the victim of some incurable form of persecution mania and had not blown up the figure of his tormentor to its present proportions in his own imagination (just possible, he supposed, fingering the paw in his pocket, but very unlikely), he was no longer at all sure that it would be correct to drag this poor young person into the affair. She seemed to have enough trouble on her hands already. She had spoken of the Catcher so fondly, too. What was it she had said? The image of his father? He stole a glance at the photograph of the fair, handsome, young carabiniere in its polished silver frame, and tried – unsuccessfully – to trace the resemblance. No, he decided, it would not do to tell the mother. She would either believe him and be upset by it, or disbelieve and remain equally upset. And anyway, he didn't really think that a simple, homely woman like this would be much help. The Catcher had foxed an

64

expert adversary like himself for months now, and would make mincemeat of this easier prey were she ever to set herself against him. Besides, the relationship between them seemed relatively untroubled at present – serene almost, from the way she had spoken – and it would be kinder to leave it that way. If the father had been alive, it would have been a different matter, maybe; but as things stood he felt he had no right to unburden himself at her expense: a duty, in fact, not to do so.

Stuffing the paw (which a night in the canal had done little to improve) firmly into his pocket and refusing the seat that he had been offered a second time, he murmured depreciatively: 'Oh, it was nothing really. Just a little matter between your son and myself. Nothing to bother you with at all. He has been throwing stones at my window and making it a little difficult for me to get on with my studies in the evenings, that's all. It's hardly worth mentioning.'

The mother looked mildly shocked: 'Peste, peste,' she said affectionately, 'I certainly *will* mention it, and you can be sure it won't happen again. So that's what he gets up to in his room at night! Well, did you ever! I told you he was high-spirited. Please forgive him, Professore, just this once, and I promise it won't happen again. I'm sure he didn't mean any harm.'

Joseph said nothing, but patted the girl's hand reassuringly by way of an answer (his sympathy with her was genuine enough, for bad as it was to have a boy like this as an enemy, he felt it was worse still to have him as a son), and took his leave.

So the Catcher had a double life, he thought grimly to himself as he made his way slowly down the stairway again and out into the welcome splatter of the rain: model son of an upright, fond and quite everyday family; keen, high-spirited pupil at school; and, in his leisure, cruel, sophisticated cat-killer and professional incubus to a poor old man like himself. He drew out the paw and stroked it thoughtfully before throwing it aside. Well, well, well. If there was no getting at him through his family, then he must tackle him personally, face to face, and that was all there was to it. Not that he liked the idea, mind you, not that he liked it at all.

VIII

L ET US leave Joseph to wrestle alone with his problems for a
while and take another bird's-eye look at him two weeks
later. He has been very busy in the interval: he has pulled
himself together as best he can and has made headway with his
testament, has graced it with a few well-constructed riddles,
built in one important piece of information in the form of a
two-tiered acrostic, another in the form of a specular rebus, and
so on, and has even gone to the trouble of designing an ana-
morphic sentence which, unless righted by the aid of a tubular
mirror, seems just a rather clumsy drawing of a whirlpool. He
has enjoyed this part of his work and has progressed fast,
although he has not yet got round to solving the vexed question
of the safety device. He has also managed to clean up the
summary and to make a dozen or so quite presentable copies of
it, in readiness for the informal but, he hopes and thinks, decisive
meeting which Trevisan has so kindly brought about for him
(without, it must be stressed, realizing exactly what subject it is
that Joseph is to speak on) and which is very shortly to take place.
On top of all this activity, and despite it, his physique is still
mysteriously holding out. He is rather proud of this and pleased
with himself for having ignored what medical advice he received
(he has his own theories about organisms, as about so many
other things), although he fully realizes at the same time that
this lull or respite is due to chance alone, cannot last, and should
not therefore cheer him.

In the mornings, to be honest, it does not cheer him at all.

With each daily return to consciousness the knowledge hits him – and hits him punctually, afresh and hard – and he lies quite still under the bedclothes and listens closely to his body, much as if it were an antique clock he has been cautioned not to buy on account of its unreliability. There it is, still ticking, though. He draws a slow breath, to see if the pain in his chest has worsened: no, it is there, but no stronger than before. He gingerly tries a cough to see if he can still control it: no worse and no more intense than the previous day. He draws a deeper breath and begins slowly and more contentedly to flex his limbs. So he is not as indifferent to death as he would have himself believe. But this is something we have guessed already.

Today he may be thinking of it again, despite himself. The scene is that of a small, flat island in the middle of a sheet of water which stretches out on all sides like a well-pinned tarpaulin – thick, dark, flat and faintly greasy. San Francesco del Deserto. Joseph's favourite island. A mist hangs low on the water-line, so that the development of the tarpaulin cannot be traced, and there is no telling where the mainland may lie, or whether there are other islands in the neighbourhood. A faint chug of engines now and again would seem to indicate that there are, but as far as the senses are directly concerned there is nothing but the one tiny island, one building on it – a monastery – and some way from the building, seated on a large stone, a solitary figure, fingertips pressed to temples and wearing a rather sad expression on his face. History's first successful magician. Poor Joseph Kestler.

Perhaps, though, despite the sepulchral quiet, despite the forlorn way he is sitting there, huddled into the folds of his threadbare overcoat, despite the grim, grey lap of the water round his toes, he isn't really sad at all. Perhaps he is, quite to the contrary, thinking excitedly about the big event which lies ahead when he will at last be able to expound his cherished theories on practical cabala to a small, select group of well-disposed hearers (well-disposed, that is, if Trevisan has done his homework properly, and if his and Joseph's criteria of 'rightness' coincide). So perhaps he is rehearsing in his mind the short opening speech he has prepared for them, or going over the last-minute details of his little experiment. He has not, as was to be expected, managed to find a locust anywhere and has had to fall back instead on a slightly bigger sort of animal. The choice has been difficult and narrow, the main limits being laid down by the Ugaritic language itself, or rather by the known range of its lexicon. Joseph has combed through all available texts in search of a substitute — a guinea-pig, as it were, for the experiment; but unfortunately, surviving samples of Ugaritic writing, dealing as they principally do with the grandiose themes of warfare and sacrifice, make scarce mention of any of the smaller species of animal. Not only is the word for guinea-pig missing from their lists, but also those for cat (which, as we have seen, would have come in very useful for other things, besides the experiment), rat, mouse, fly, spider and canary. There is a generic term for birds, and a more precise one for eagles and other birds of prey; there are also plenty of terms for beasts of utility value in an early pastoral society such as ox, mule, ram, heifer, lamb, calf, buffalo, sheep, cow, bull, goat and so forth, which Joseph has reluctantly had to exclude for reasons of space and fittingness (for he rightly feels that he cannot very well turn up for the encounter in the company of any of these). In a less domestic vein, the chronicles make mention also of snakes, sharks, lions and deer, which on equally sound reasoning he has had to exclude. It is all very frustrating. During the research it has even crossed his mind once or twice to give up the idea of animal experiment altogether and to settle instead for a less showy maybe but less dicey test on a more tractable organism. To this end he has spent quite some time looking for a potted mandrake — the mandrake being one of the very few plants which crop up in the texts, no doubt on account of its supposed fertility value. He has not managed to find one, however, and has finally lighted on the idea of using a dog (by far the most simple solution and one that he ought to have cottoned on to straight away, there being a very pretty line in the funeral poem sung by Keret's daughter Thitmanet which runs: 'We shall cry outside your dwelling-place like a howling dog, like a stray dog outside your burial place'). A dog, or, better still — so as to get as near the mark as possible and leave little or no margin for error – a stray, and he has asked his fellow lodger Emilio to find one for him.

So much for three of his tasks. The fourth and most unpleasant one – that of thwarting the Catcher – has not met with the same success: hardly surprising, when it has not been tackled with anything like the same zeal. He has twice forced himself to lie in wait for his repellent little namesake with the idea of accosting him face to face as he makes his way home from school; but each time, for different reasons, he has failed dismally in the carrying-out of his plan. Perhaps I had better explain in more detail.

The first time he failed because he was simply not quick enough. He chose what he thought was an ideal place to wait, standing just inside the framer's workshop with his back to the square, and keeping a look-out in a mirror which conveniently reflected the approach for him so that he could cover the Catcher's movements without being seen himself. (Or so he hoped.) But the mirror must have alerted the Catcher too, for when at last he drew alongside and Joseph swung purposefully round to face him, he found himself confronting nothing but a swirl of displaced air. The child had ducked under his outstretched arm, and had darted with incredible speed into the middle of the square where he stood poised like an antelope for a second dart, smiling a hospitable little smile in Joseph's direction and signalling with a toss of the head that he was ready for the chase. So there was no getting him that way.

The next time, though, Joseph was more careful, and by standing behind a pillar in the dank entrance hall of the palazzo itself and waiting until the child was within inches of him, he was able to make a successful grab and take a firm hold of his satchel straps from behind. Hanging on to them tightly to prevent him escaping, and twisting the boy round to face him, he began to speak. He spoke levelly at first, reasoning with the boy and appealing to his sense of decency, but when all he got in return was the smooth, unblinking stare of a waxwork he became more heated. He shook the little bony shoulders until the head rattled on top of them – still with no change of its facial expression –

and began to use threats. Finally, slipping from anger to unwisdom, his voice cracked with emotion, he did what he had most strongly resolved not to do and resorted to pleading. All to no avail. The child heard him out in silence – quite politely, in that he made no attempt to wriggle free or to resist the shaking – and then, when he seemed satisfied that Joseph had finished, merely parted his lips in a grin to reveal an ornate, steel, straightening device over his teeth, so weird that it caused Joseph to start and slacken his hold, slipped from his grasp and ran lightly up the stairs. On the landing he turned, gave the metallic teeth another airing, and said in a reedy, even voice tinged with what sounded like scorn, or even disappointment: 'La credevo più forte.' I thought you were stronger. With this he disappeared up the stairs, the satchel bouncing behind him; leaving Joseph stunned and speechless, and with nothing gained from the meeting except a nasty, cloying smell on his hands where they had touched the shoulders.

So you see, poor fellow, he has suffered, if not total defeat, at least a major set-back on the Catcher front and has made a fool of himself in the process. He is angry with himself over this, as can be expected, and ashamed of himself for being angry and for being ashamed. His feelings are layered and complex. They are further complicated by the fact that he is not sure any more that he is dealing with a cruel little boy at all, but has begun to query the steadier and more cautious doctrines which he has believed in up to now, and to think that the Catcher is some kind of evil spirit or other which has been sent to plague him and to disrupt his work. The violence of these feelings or imaginings or what-have-you of his, and the shaky premises on which they are based, cause him to worry at the same time about the state of his mental well-being. Is he, he asks himself anxiously from time to time, becoming a little unhinged in the upper storey? Is the disease affecting his mind now as well as his body? Is he going mad? Has he perhaps always been mad? And does the famous testament, then, contain nothing but the rantings of a lunatic? Then he shifts up a level and asks himself whether it could not be that these very doubts which plague him are yet another wile of the enemy's, engineered with Machiavellian skill to prevent him from getting on with his work. And so it goes on, in a mounting spiral of anxiety; and on he works, despite it. This, of course, may be another thing he is thinking about as he sits there alone on the island, wrapped about by an insufficiently warm overcoat and by wisps of thickening fog. It is a point that we might do well to examine for ourselves. We said at the beginning, when discussing the positive elements in his character, that he might turn out to be ingenious, but I am no longer sure that this can be argued for very convincingly. His delight in the world, the care he takes never to interfere with other people's lives, his fondness for animals, his courage and so forth — all these are very well and good and one cannot help admiring him for them; but it cannot be glossed over or ignored that he has, on the other hand, spent his entire existence and all his gifts and all his energy in the pursuit of a very questionable objective indeed: magical power over animate objects. Even if we are prepared to forgive him his latest dotty theory about the evil spirit, and put it down to tiredness or stress, we still have to face it that he thinks — quite seriously and consideredly thinks — that he has discovered a key to the original language that was one of God's first and most generous gifts to man. The language — to put it more clearly, if a little over-simply — with which Adam Kadmon, the original man, baptized the brand-new furniture of the world. As related in the well-known Bible story: '. . . and whatsoever Adam called every living creature, that was the name thereof.' That story. That language. And although Joseph thinks of it more eruditely as the 'Ursprache' and gives only a smiling credit to its connection with the Book of Genesis, he definitely thinks that this language exists, and thinks moreover that once correctly translated into numerical values it is sufficient to yield a kind of energy or power of its own over the thus named and numbered objects.

Put nakedly like this, as a theory it seems a real paradigm of crackpottery (although one must bear in mind, as Joseph himself constantly does, that it is a theory which throughout the ages — off and on, of course, but until only very recently much more on than off – has attracted the attention of quite a number of first-class brains). All the same, his championship of it is more than a little disconcerting. Let us put it this way – in pure dilemma form again, incidentally: either he is not clever, or else he is; and if he *is* clever, then he has made very silly use of all his cleverness and is therefore not clever at all. There would seem to be no way round this, not even, using Joseph's favourite route, through its horns. It is an inescapable logical truth; and if the case of his cleverness is to be argued for at all, then it cannot be from here but must be from a position way upstream of the dilemma. One must ask oneself, that is, a prior question and have the humility and/or audacity to say simply: 'Yes, but what if the theory works?'

What indeed? We might then, who knows, have to re-examine not only the question of Joseph's ingenuity, but many others along with it. What if he can *prove* that it works – not once, but time and time again? And not only on raindrops, locusts and an obliging dog, but on all the items he can find a Ugaritic term for – items which, apart from sacrificial livestock and the odd wild beast or so, include also such eminently useful things as clouds, rivers, seas, stars and so forth. What if it turned out that his strangely acquired power had a hold over all these? There is even a Ugaritic term for soldiers, come to think of it (although for human beings, of course, you might have to know the proper name as well). Oh no. The range of application is definitely not as narrow as it may seem.

Luckily, though, such speculation is idle even before it is ridiculous. The experiment is shortly to take place in front of reliable and impartial witnesses, and there is no need for us to make up our minds until we have seen how the University professors react. It is comforting to be able to rely on their more expert opinion. Let's just hope they won't be too hard on him if he fails – or even if he succeeds for that matter – since clever or not, fool, dupe or genius as he may be, he really doesn't deserve it.

IX

THE MOMENT he got back to his lodgings, Joseph knew that his trip to San Francesco had been a mistake – a mawkish lapse of self-discipline which he would regret. His favourite place, his favourite view, the last visit he was likely to make to it, and the mist had risen so rapidly on his arrival that he had been able to see nothing of anything, but had had to wait there dismally as if marooned in a plate of soup until the boat had returned to fetch him. So much for nostalgia. Now it would take him hours to get warm again, and to make matters worse his coat had picked up a sharp, marshy smell that would be hard to get rid of in time for the big occasion on the next afternoon. A shame, when he had so wanted to look and feel his best and make a good impression from the start. Who was it that Trevisan had said would be coming? A professor of Semitic languages, one Siani or Diani; a philosopher of languages by the name of Chianese – Neapolitan, and rumoured to be something of a nominalist; two mathematical cronies of Trevisan's, unrelated but sharing the common surname of Monti; a Dr Martis, a Renaissance scholar – young, female, and destined, so Trevisan had said pregnantly, to go far; and a Jesuit from Padua whose life was devoted to the counting of word frequencies and whose name Joseph had not managed to catch. That made six of them, and by the sound of it, all rather high-powered and eminent in their particular fields. Hardly the sort of public you could face up to with aplomb in an overcoat smelling of swamp, he feared. Trevisan had run through the list with him over the telephone in hushed tones, evidently struck by his success in organizing the little gathering: they were to meet, he whispered proudly, in the University itself, in a small but well-appointed room that had been specially lent them thanks to a virtuoso performance of string-pulling and weight-throwing on his part. It was lucky he had hit on the idea of the dog, reflected Joseph feelingly as he thought back on his friend's athletic-sounding achievement. Just imagine if he had had to enter the precincts of the University, as it had at one time seemed he might, with a robust animal in tow; not only ailing and dressed in a smelly overcoat, but with a sheep or goat, or worse still a cow, on a tether. It would have been downright discourteous towards Trevisan after all his kindness, prejudicial to the furniture, and would have made a poor first impression all round.

Fortunately, though, apart from the ill-timed trip to the island, his preparations had been well carried out and thorough. The summary was ready; he had memorized his address, cleaned his shoes and collected his laundry. He had bought cough-drops and after-shave lotion. He had also remembered to buy himself fresh fruit, a bottle of mineral water and two small slices of cheese, so as to spare himself the bother of going out to a restaurant, but to eat light and early instead and then to retire to the relative comfort of his bed for a similarly lightweight read. Material for this last part of his programme had been the hardest to obtain, but the bookstore had finally responded to his timid request – 'Something light,' he had whispered confidentially to the assistant, not wanting to betray his ignorance of the genre, so total that he hardly knew which part of the shop to inspect in order to find it – with a strange-looking volume, its cover acrawl with human limbs and locks, which, after his initial surprise, he had now begun to feel mildly curious about.

Yes, the preparations were almost completed: the only important thing that remained still to be settled was the question of the dog. And seeing that this was such an essential part of his equipment, he felt he had better check immediately, and make quite sure Emilio had managed to find what was wanted. Strays were plentiful in Italy as a rule, of course – only too plentiful –

but it might turn out that now that he really needed one there would be none for the finding. Hurriedly exchanging his sodden set of clothes for a merely damp one, he padded off down the corridor in his slippers to enquire.

The room was unusually silent for this time of evening – a time when the basset horn was apt to boom with fierce, pre-prandial zest. There was no sound of practising, nor of the disheartened muttering which so often accompanied it, nor any sound of occupation at all, yet the light was on.

Joseph knocked gently. Getting no reply he knocked again, this time a little louder. A hiss came from behind the door, followed by a low, indistinct whisper. Taking this as an invitation to enter, he turned the handle and poked his head cautiously round the edge of the door, to find Emilio seated bolt upright on the very edge of the bed, cradling a small, curled puppy in his lap. He shrugged his shoulders and smiled at Joseph to indicate that he couldn't get up, or talk, for fear of waking it.

Joseph stood and stared, and stared again. Until then he hadn't really thought of the object of his experiment as an animal. He had just thought of it as an object. Where it was to come from, where and how long it was to stay, were details he had not taken into account, beyond a vague mention to Emilio that he would be needing it for a day or two at the outside; in fact, they had not even crossed his mind, so busy had it been with other things. Now that he set eyes on the creature, though, he realized that he had made a mistake in this and had set about the enterprise far too lightly. For it was a truly exceptional little creature that Emilio had found: not an object at all, but a warm, breathing, soft, little semicircle of apricot-coloured and very individual animal. Its fur – more like a seal's than a dog's – stuck out at right angles in shiny, pointed tufts, thickening with the development of the body and ending in a blunt tail, soft and fluffy as a feather duster. The whiskers too were thick and seal-like, and vibrated, as did the nose set between them, to the peaceful rhythm of its snoring. Joseph stood in the doorway and gazed, noting these details with an almost tender approval; at the same time admitting to himself worriedly that, although it would do nicely for the experiment, this was certainly not the sort of animal he could use light-heartedly just the once , as he had the locusts, and then dismiss from his life by putting it back where it had been found. No. It was warm, and young, and vital, and beautiful (a set of qualities so different from his own that he could not help smiling a little over the contrast), and there was no question but that it must be cared for. No, no, no. Dismissal was unthinkable. It was the sort of animal he knew he would very rapidly become attached to and feel responsible for. Responsible – that was the snag. In fact, no sooner had this thought crossed his mind than the sense of responsibility concretized and settled heavily on his shoulders like a cloak, and with a sigh of contented resignation he stepped into the room and closed the door behind him. So be it, he thought calmly as he did so; another problem, another tie, another commitment, another encroachment on his dwindling stock of time, and yet in its way such a novel one that it had a curiously welcome feel about it.

True to his expectations, the rest of Joseph's evening was, in fact, devoted entirely to the shouldering of this new responsibility. Together with an equally captivated Emilio, he shopped for dog-food, drinking-bowls, a basket, a leash and collar, surprised at the sudden and steep rise of the animal's needs. Emilio seemed to know more about the matter. It was he who suggested a brush and metal comb for its toilet, and he who remembered to ask about vaccinations and vitamins and how to obtain a licence. He also did his best to dissuade Joseph (who had by now entered very much into the spirit of the thing and, egged on by the shopkeeper, had chosen a flea-collar and a very expensive reversible cushion that could be switched from cotton to wool for the cold weather) from buying a synthetic bone for the puppy to chew on. It must, he explained earnestly, be allowed to adopt a fetish of its own choosing; he doubted its personality would ever mature otherwise. If left to itself, it would probably settle for something of Joseph's – a slipper maybe, or a book. At which Joseph gave him a worried look and added the bone firmly to the growing pile of purchases.

Besides the shopping, though, and the feeding, and a closely supervised outing to cater for its other bodily needs, it was, of course, the matter of a name for the dog that took up the best part of the evening, Joseph being understandably convinced that a name was something to be discovered, not merely given. By ten p.m. the field had been whittled down to something definitely bisyllabic, starting with La or Lo – that much, he said pensively, crouched on his hands and knees and wheezing with the effort of keeping pace with the puppy the better to observe its reactions, that much any fool could see. But a further fifteen minutes of trial and error were to elapse before the name itself was identified.

In the silence that followed a spate of disappointing Lallos and Lottos, and just as Joseph was beginning to have a serious rethink about the number of syllables, Emilio suddenly clapped his hand to his forehead and said: 'Lapo!' The puppy froze to an attentive standstill, cocked its head to one side, and looked at both men with an unmistakable stare of recognition. Joseph beamed at Emilio and Emilio beamed back. 'That's what comes of knowing your Dante, Joe,' he explained modestly; 'Guido, I would that Lapo, thou and I, led by some strong enchantment, might ascend a magic ship . . . Lapo Gianni. A friend of Dante's.'

'Lapo,' echoed Joseph, and the puppy trotted obediently towards him. 'Lapo,' he repeated solemnly, placing his thumb on the dog's forehead and making a small downward motion, as if drawing a mark there. 'A friend of Dante's, and now a friend of ours.'

The question settled, he rose stiffly to his feet and with a quick little smile to both of them, returned to his room alone. It cost him quite an effort, as he felt he would really have preferred to keep the dog for the night himself. But apart from the fact that it seemed wrong somehow to bind it too closely to such a precarious master, he knew it was important that he be able to tell his audience with a clear conscience that he had had no previous contact with the animal. Otherwise he would lay himself open to the accusation of cheating. In fact, to ensure doubly against this, he decided that not only must he keep a rigorous distance until the moment of the experiment, but must also limit himself during the experiment itself to use of the Ugaritic class-name for strays (since, strictly speaking, he shouldn't be in possession of the proper name at all) and must work out Lapo's individual number for his private satisfaction alone.

With this diverting aim in mind, and arming himself with paper, pencil, and his more reliable revolving-wheel, he went contentedly to his awaiting supper and then to bed. The evening had tired him, he had to admit, but it had been one of the happiest he had spent in a long while. Whether it had been the novelty of having another living being besides himself to look after, or the pleasure of having someone to talk to on an easy subject for a change, he didn't know, but his mind had certainly been taken off his worries. Come to think of it, what with the shopping and the naming and the rest, he hadn't even had time to get cold feet about the momentous meeting next day.

Before he dropped off to sleep, however, two worrying thoughts did manage to worm their way into his mind. The first – the question of getting round the landlady and persuading her to accept a pet in her establishment – was one he decided upon reflection that he had better leave to Emilio. Emilio's halo of hedgehog hair and the state of his jerseys brought out, or so he always claimed, parental instincts in members of both sexes, and although Joseph could hardly credit his landlady with maternal ones, he felt that there might conceivably be a scattering of avuncular, or similar, promptings somewhere in her make-up and that these it would be Emilio's task to locate. The second, with a new and painful twist added to it, and one that he must deal with personally, was, of course, the problem of the Catcher.

Since his debacle on the staircase, the enemy had been strangely quiet. Joseph had expected a triumphant follow-up: more paws on the ledge outside his window, more victims in the street below, a message maybe, or a derisive face confronting him from across the way. But there had been nothing of this. Instead, there had been a lull in hostilities. A suspension. Silence. Much as if, conscious by now of his opponent's weakness, the Catcher knew he had only to wait for his mistakes in order to win. That was what it felt like to Joseph anyway: as if, like a patient, wily spider, the enemy had completed the active part of the offensive and was crouching immobile in the background, waiting for a false move on his part. And now, of course, he had made one. Punctually, compliantly, with Lapo's arrival he had opened up another serious flaw in his crumbling defences.

Wide awake now, he pounded angrily at the pillow and then struggled to a sitting position to continue his worrying more energetically from there. For what would the Catcher do, and what not do, he asked himself miserably, once he had found out about Lapo? Lapo in the Catcher's hands. Lapo on the Catcher's hook. The mere thought of it was enough to make him queasy with anxiety. It must not happen, and that was all there was to it. The Catcher must never know of the dog's existence; or, if this could not be hidden from him – and at such close quarters it was more or less impossible – then he must never suspect that the dog was Joseph's property or was connected to him in any way.

His hands prickling with sweat, he groped in the darkness for his magician's dressing-gown, draped it clumsily around him and hurried down the darkened passage towards Emilio's room: what he must do, of course – without alarming him unduly or revealing too much – was to warn his friend about this immediately, before it was too late.

The light was still on and Emilio was sitting on the floor by the basket playing with the puppy, in much the same position as he had been all evening. He started and gave a somewhat sheepish smile, as if expecting to be accused of trying to steal a march during Joseph's absence.

'He's just not sleepy, Joe, I'm afraid,' he explained by way of excuse. 'I have tried putting *him* in *his* bed and *me* in *mine*, and I have tried both together in mine, but this is the only way he seems to like. Maybe he's used to company at nights and is feeling a bit lonely.'

'Ah,' said Joseph thoughtfully, eyeing the creature fondly, and wishing more fervidly than ever that his conscience would only allow him to keep the puppy with him for the night. 'Not sleeping? Well, that's no problem.' He crossed over to the basket, put his head in his hands for a few seconds in intense concentration and then stooped down and, lifting the silky flap of the outer ear, whispered a short sequence of words. The effect was instantaneous. The puppy twitched the receiving ear and gave a drowsy nod, its head sank on to the two neatly aligned forepaws, its eyes closed and, after a quick lick of its nose, it fell into the soft, light, routine breathing of profound sleep.

Emilio gave an astonished laugh. 'A little magic,' said Joseph unassumingly, placing a biscuit on the dog's nose to test the depth of its slumber. He bent down again to run a finger through the hillocks of apricot fur. 'Emilio,' he added hesitantly, staring hard at the placid, good-natured expression in his eyes and willing it to heedfulness. 'One other important thing I forgot to mention. It is agreed that I prepare the meals, then, and you deal with the outings, but I am afraid I must insist that on no account you take Lapo into the square. I know the trees would be handy,' he went on earnestly, 'and I know that it is asking you to make a detour each time, but promise me that you will take him elsewhere on his walks. Take him anywhere but there. And keep him on the lead when you are anywhere near the pensione.'

Emilio looked puzzled, but nodded an unquestioning agreement. He placed a large, hot hand on Joseph's shoulder: 'We look after him OK, Joe,' he said, 'niente paura.' There is nothing to fear. But unfortunately Joseph had reason to believe otherwise.

X

I T WAS drizzling when Joseph with Lapo trotting alongside set out for Ca' Foscari, the large, grey-brown Gothic palace which housed one of the principal faculties of Venice's now rather depleted University, and where the meeting was to take place. To avoid the Catcher seeing them together, he had left the pensione alone and had waited at a pre-arranged spot some distance away for Emilio to bring the dog to him, but this simple precaution did not seem to be working very well.

The first stage of the journey was uneventful. He went ahead slowly and cautiously, stopping every now and then to check any suspicious sound or movement and to keep an eye on the few passers-by who like himself had braved the chill, listless hour of the early afternoon, but noticed nothing to worry him particularly; the only moving objects he saw, in fact, being a few pigeons, a cat, two plastic-swathed Japanese tourists, and a small band of students who surged past him gaily, laughing, gesticulating and eating sandwiches the crumbs of which flew carelessly behind them and dotted their path like a trail of confetti.

As he left the sheltered streets of his own neighbourhood, though, and crossed into the wide, open expanse of Campo San Barnaba, he heard a quick, scuttling footfall echoing his own and, turning rapidly, caught sight of a darting movement on the far side of the square behind him: a patch of shadow that sped towards the cover of the church like a bat, and nestled there against the wall. Holding tight to Lapo's leash, he waited a little to get a better look at it, narrowing his eyes and trying to make out the exact spot at which it had halted; but the small shadow had now blended into the larger, denser one thrown by the building and he was no longer able to see it clearly, nor even to decide whether it really could have been what he feared it was, or whether it might in fact have been nothing but a bird or a bat after all.

Unsettled by this, and already badly on edge about the coming meeting, he covered the remaining distance to the University walking almost crabwise, straining eyes and ears for further signs of his follower; and with a quaky, vulnerable feeling just below his diaphragm as if he were heading for an examination, or an ordeal, instead of a conference of his own devising. When he finally reached the courtyard of Ca' Foscari he could hardly bring himself to go forward at all and, grateful for the propulsion it gave him, he hung on to the lead and let the dog draw him on and into the building itself.

Excepting Trevisan, he and Lapo were the first to arrive. The Italian greeted Joseph warmly, but seemed a trifle piqued that his friend should have seen fit to turn up for the distinguished occasion in the company of a dog. 'A new companion?' he queried, his eyes behind their thick lenses blinking fast in disapproval. 'Was there no other place for you to deposit it?' He gave a rapid glance towards the doorway to keep a look-out for eventual arrivals, and his hands twiddled on the back of a chair in nervous expectation. He had, he pointed out to Joseph proudly, made the seating arrangements personally. In fact, if truth be told, he had made them, and then unmade them, and then remade them all over again in what he hoped was now an optimal fashion.

Joseph nodded his thanks. 'The dog is party to the experiment,' he explained apologetically but firmly, 'so there can be no question of, as you put it, "depositing" him elsewhere.' He gave Lapo a reassuring pat. 'He is an essential part of my equipment, and that, I am afraid, caro Dottore, is that. You see, when I have finished speaking, I shall place him in full view of the audience, and begin the experiment proper by . . .'

Trevisan, however, was no longer paying full attention. He

had spotted a hesitant figure on the threshold and was now bustling towards it, shattering as he did so the optimal layout of the chairs. He returned soon after like a triumphant hunter, having drawn into the room a small, white-haired priest, the sleeve of whose cassock he was still grasping, and introduced Joseph to this first arrival by a flush of impressive titles – 'my friend the meritorious Professore', 'eminente studioso', 'scholar of this and that and the other' – which Joseph had difficulty in relating to himself. Fearful lest Trevisan in his enthusiasm had given him too glowing a build-up, he ventured a timid disclaimer, and as he spoke, the Jesuit's name escaped him for the second time. Padre Tommaso Something-or-other. An operatic-sounding name. Could it have been Bellini? Or Cherubini?

The priest held out a soft, scented hand, withdrew it almost immediately and stood in silence, eyeing the floor, causing Joseph to wonder sympathetically whether the word-counting was something that went on all the time even when he was off-duty. If so, then it would surely be kinder to speak as little as possible himself and make things easier for the poor man.

Trevisan hovered between them, a hand on the shoulder of each, and smiled encouragingly from face to face. 'Padre Tommaso is very interested in your theories about the cabala, is that not so, Padre?' he prodded encouragingly after a lengthy interval, his attention still claimed by the doorway. 'He was telling me just the other evening that not so very long ago, here in Venice there used to be a curious, rather sinister kind of figure . . .'

At this point, however, the priest, reinforcing Joseph's suspicions about the word-counting, dropped disconcertingly to his knees and intoned the words 'cabalà, cabalà, cabalà', in a gentle sing-song. Nor, more disconcertingly still, was it clear for quite some time that this was intended merely as an overture towards the puppy. As soon as Joseph realized what he was about, however, he relaxed and warmed to the man instantly, and began to explain to him the little that he knew of the dog's history, and his reasons for bringing him along. To this the priest made no reply, but gave Joseph a quick, searching look, and rolling a tuft of dog-hair between thumb and finger, continued to intone quietly under his breath.

Trevisan in his role of master of ceremonies looked on worriedly as this exchange – or lack of one – took place; but before he was able to get his charges to behave with the decorum he would have liked, his scrutiny of the doorway was rewarded by the appearance of other guests and, turning his back on the two elderly men, he sped welcomingly towards them. The room, already cramped, seemed to get smaller still as a group of seven or eight participants entered in a rush, chattering, laughing, and looking about them expectantly as if they had been invited to a party.

Falling victim to a sudden and violent bout of stage fright, and trying in the face of it to hold fast to his much-needed concentration, Joseph had no time to notice anything but the group itself, and was scarcely able to attach to any particular member any of the names he had been so careful to memorize beforehand. He managed to identify the two mathematicians on account of their size, remembering that Trevisan had referred to them jokingly as the 'Monti-celli', the tiny mountains, and – with difficulty – the one female present, but no others apart from these. They were younger than he had expected, and there were more of them, and they were noisier. What was more, they all seemed to know each other and, apart from a brisk shake of his hand on entry and a word of greeting, to be keener on renewing their already extant interrelationships than forging new ones with himself. None of them acknowledged Lapo.

When Trevisan had finally got them quiet and seated, therefore, and had made a short, official presentation, explaining (as far as he was able) why it was that they were assembled there and adding regretfully that there were to be no refreshments, it was the priest whom Joseph singled out as earpiece. It was to him that he handed out the carefully prepared copies of the summary to be passed on to the others; it was to him that he spoke throughout; and it was from him – from the medley of expressions which crossed his pink and white countenance tinging it to eventual saturation, and which spanned interest, surprise, consternation, incredulity and shock in that order – that he was able to tell the extent of his failure.

Mercifully, it was all over quite quickly. The copies were handed round and Joseph waited in courteous silence for his audience to acquaint themselves a little with the contents, filling in the time by fetching a table from a corner of the room on which he could stand Lapo so that everyone could see him properly, and by tying the puppy's lead firmly to the leg of the table. Then he took another look at his audience. The summary did not seem to be going down very well. There was coughing and a shifting of chairs, to which Lapo added by giving a pull on the lead and jerking the table half a metre towards the nearest chair. Then came more coughing and a giggle from the female scholar.

This did not worry Joseph much, though, and keeping his eyes fixed steadfastly on the more receptive gaze of the dog-loving priest, he began quietly and simply to deliver the short speech he had prepared. Apart from a minor disturbance when one of the mathematicians rose and with a whispered excuse to Trevisan left the room, and a second interruption some moments later when an usher entered on tiptoe with an urgent message for the second mathematician, who also rose and made his exit, the speech was well received. Better received than the summary, anyway, Joseph thought, judging by the litmus indicator of the priest's colouring which was now a quiet shade of rose-petal. He had spoken modestly and well and had held his audience's attention, and now had them waiting – this time in a silence unbroken by throat-clearings and a stillness unruffled by the crossing of legs and the flutter of handkerchiefs – for the experiment to begin.

He had, of course, long debated on what would most impress this select little band of onlookers, and despite Trevisan's re-assurances as to their 'rightness', had never been so naive as to imagine that they would be anything other than deeply critical, if not downright sceptical, of the views he was to put before them. He had not expected, it was true, that their scepticism would be so strong as to goad them into rudeness (for that was how he interpreted the hasty departure of the two mathematicians), but he had known all along that they would be a hard bunch to convince. Now that he was directly facing them, however, he slightly regretted his choice. Had he had a few locusts, for example, he thought wistfully as he ran his eyes over the numerous pairs now expectantly trained on him, although of less impact from a scenic point of view, it would have made his task easier. He could have repeated the experiment as many times over as he had locusts. He could have got them to gyrate in pairs, maybe; or could have invited members of the audience to have a little try themselves once they had grasped the simple number technique and had proved themselves capable of the right amount of concentration. (Of course, it was unlikely they would have succeeded in this at such short notice – one *particularly* tricky point being how to have prevented them from backsliding through the various levels of concentration once they had reached them – but with his own expert guidance, not impossible.) And, although it wouldn't really have been very kind to the insects, he could also have ended up in an extremely spectacular finale by freezing the locusts rigid. All of this was out of the question with Lapo. The solution he had fallen back on, therefore, was to begin with a simple display of immobility, head-turning, eye-shutting and opening, which could be done as often as desired with no risk to the animal. He would then ask the members of the audience to make some suggestions of their own (so as they wouldn't think he had trained the dog to perform a given set of tricks); and would wind up as he had done for Emilio's benefit the evening before by lulling the puppy into a deep, induced sleep. It was not exactly the best he could do, but he hoped it would be convincing enough.

Before beginning, he gave another glance at the row of faces before him and saw with relief that, although his guests might be critical, there was no doubt about whether or not he had managed to capture their attention. All were sitting very still and bolt upright, perched without exception on the extreme edge of their chairs. The priest's face had gone pinker between the two white strips of collar and hair, and he too was craning forward to get a better view of what was going on. Trevisan, his chair placed a little apart and slightly behind the others, had replaced his usual glasses with a pince-nez and was staring straight ahead of him with wide-open eyes and an expression of probing interest, mixed with something that looked (due no doubt, thought Joseph, to the change of lenses) remarkably like indignation.

With a reassuring smile to all of them but to no one in particular, Joseph gathered Lapo in his arms, placed him gently on the table where he sat obediently but not without a certain amount of wiggling and wagging of the tail, and, turning his back on the audience with a gesture of apology, plunged his head in his hands and strove for profound and immediate concentration.

Afterwards he wondered if this, from the point of view of showmanship, had not been a mistake. When he turned round again, in fact, through the heavy curtain of his concentration – almost trance-like in its intensity – he could tell that a change had taken place in the spectators. As in a game of grandmother's footsteps, the setting, array and mood had shifted into a subtly different pattern. The chairs seemed fewer and closer, the faces less well-disposed, and the priest's, in particular, very pink indeed. But ignoring this – blotting out everything but the puppy from the field of his attention – he went calmly ahead with the experiment.

No sooner had he whispered the number than he knew the experiment was to be the best and greatest that he had ever performed. The animal came to him immediately, its eyes unblinkingly fixed upon his own, and he could feel its surrender and wholesale submission almost as if it had been a solid gift that had been put in his grasp. The awareness of his power flooded joyfully through him. He could feel it in his hands, in his head and even in the pit of his stomach. It ran through him like a current. Yes; more definitely than the raindrop, more – much more – than the locust, this little being was his. His to hold in existence, his to manoeuvre, and like a docile lump of clay in a sculptor's hands, to mould into any form that he liked. Murmuring the ciphered name again, he began cautiously and with a sense of almost sacred respect, to take over the functioning of the pliant little body placed at his disposal.

When he had finished, keeping his head well bowed and his eyes tight shut so as not to lose his concentration, he held his hand in the air to signal a pause, and waited for the audience to make their requests as they had been asked to do at the beginning. When none came, he risked his concentration to the point of asking them to do so a second time. His words came out with difficulty, flat and jerky, and sounded to him as if they had been said by someone else. There was still no response. Not wanting to leave the puppy in his unnatural state for long – he was sitting a little askew, one leg sticking out stiffly and one ear raised and bent like that of a rubber toy – Joseph was on the point of loosening him up again when a voice rapped out in tones of unmistakable anger: 'You want a suggestion? Get it to jump out of the window, then.'

It was Trevisan. Joseph's concentration snapped; the sense of giddy omnipotence drained out of him, leaving, like dirty bath-water, only a rim to mark the one-time high it had reached; and deprived of it, unsustained by it, he plummeted painfully down to earth and to awareness of his surroundings.

Lapo yawned, stretched, shook himself and began to scratch at his ear as if nothing had happened. The room, Joseph noted in dismay, was empty save for Trevisan and a by now fuchsine-faced Padre Tommaso. He was hard put to know exactly what had happened, so sure had he been of his success, but the hastily abandoned chairs spoke only too clearly: his audiences had walked out on him – deserted him. Most likely they had not even waited for him to finish the experiment, but had left in the early stages while his back had been turned. On the floor, crumpled and strewn, lay the copies of the summary, and for some reason this detail stung him hardest of all: they might at least, he thought, at least, at least have had the civility to take them with them and throw them away elsewhere.

As he began to realize the enormity of the snub he had received, colour seeped into his own face too. He coughed painfully and the handkerchief came away from his mouth stained with blood. Pocketing it shamefacedly, he raised his head with an effort to face the two remaining members of his audience, confusedly aware as he did so that the snub had hurt him more on Trevisan's behalf than on his own. Poor Trevisan, he thought unhappily, venturing the shadow of a smile at the stony face opposite; poor, obliging Trevisan. It was he who had suffered the gravest slight, and he who would mind the most about it. Although, strange to say, from the way he was looking now, and all due allowance made for the distortion of the pince-nez, it seemed to be at himself, and not at the guests, that Trevisan's resentment was directed. What was it that he had shouted? 'Tell the dog to jump out of the window'? Now that was most unlike the Trevisan he knew. Wholly at odds with the formal and polite Trevisan he had had dealings with to date. His disappointment was understandable, of course, after all the trouble he had taken to organize things – that much must be allowed – but Joseph doubted it could justify quite such an outburst. He must set about righting things between them immediately. Hooking Lapo firmly to the table-leg once more and dragging his overcoat from under the chair where he had stowed it away earlier to conceal its mustiness, he went towards his friend, his hands spread in a gesture of bewilderment and apology.

'Caro Dottore,' he began, a smile lighting the haggard set of his features; 'caro Dottor' Trevisan, I cannot begin to tell you how sorry I am about the way our little meeting has turned out. If I had had the least suspicion of what my experiment was to provoke, I assure you that I would have spared us both the humiliation . . .' Here he broke off and watched Trevisan with anxiety. The man was trembling – quivering from head to foot; the pince-nez misted, the hair awry, the face murky, glistening and mobile as a plate of aspic. He looked to be not only resentful but very angry indeed. 'Caro amico,' Joseph went on earnestly, 'I would, please believe me, have willingly renounced . . . for all the world, I would not have wished to expose you . . .'

But Trevisan seemed hardly to be listening. Nor, though his gaze from behind the small, beaded panes of glass was trained directly to Joseph, did he appear to see him either. More than anger, he seemed to be in the grip of what Joseph could only diagnose as acute mental indigestion – indigestion which the small opening of his mouth, like the narrow end of a conglomerated funnel, could do nothing to relieve. In fact, Joseph noted with a certain interest, you could almost see the thoughts and sentences building up behind it in a pile, like so many grains of sand, or peppercorns, and wedging themselves there and sticking fast.

In this apoplectic state, he stood his ground for some seconds more, managing to give vent to nothing more cathartic than some strange hybrid noises, half-way between spitting and the clucking of a hen; then, with a final puff of exasperation, he turned on his heels and hurried from the room.

Joseph took a deep breath, closed his eyes for a moment and began mechanically to gather his papers together. He untied Lapo, carried the table back to where it had stood, straightened the row of chairs, and stooped to collect the litter of discarded summaries and to iron them out into a re-usable shape again. As things had turned out, it had been extravagant of him to run to photocopies, and it seemed a shame to waste them. One had been pounced on by Lapo and was no longer even worth ironing. He sighed and threw it back to him, thinking as he did so that it was the only copy that had served any purpose. Ah well, ah well. He must just pull himself together, he supposed. It was no use dwelling on what had happened. And no use recriminating, either. It was his own stupid fault. He should have known better. After all, what use could a University have for a magician like himself? Or for any magician, for that matter? No, he mustn't go blaming others when it was only himself that was to blame.

He watched Lapo scurry after the summary and toss it into the air, and could hardly help smiling despite himself. It was the dog's way of telling him it was time they left this frowsty atmosphere and took a walk, and he agreed with him. It was time to go. Later on, when the numbness had worn off, he supposed he would have to go back over things in a little more detail – patch up his tattered pride (luckily there was so little of it left that it wouldn't take long), practise a little salutary wound-licking and so forth, and start all over again from square one with the problem of the testament. But quietly and calmly and with no sense of drama, for nothing irreparable had taken place. Trevisan's outburst, of course; that had wounded him; and that might be a little hard to recover from. But as to the rest, he didn't really care.

He struggled into his coat, picked up Lapo's lead and made his way to the door. As he reached it, however, and was on the point of leaving, there came a light cough from behind, and a voice said gently: 'Mala tempora currunt.' Joseph started. He had forgotten about the priest. He turned slowly round to face this colourful remnant of his audience, thinking as he did so that Aristotle might have got things the wrong way round, and that it might after all be orthodoxy that did wonders for manners. This Padre Whatever-his-name-was had been the only cleric present, and he was the only one who had not walked out on him, and who had had a kind word for Lapo. From the tone of his voice, too, despite his complexion, he seemed to have kept his patience throughout. Joseph looked at him enquiringly.

'Mala tempora. Mala tempora,' the priest repeated, nodding his head up and down with a pleasant smile. 'Bad times we live in. A most unfashionable thesis, yours, if I may take the liberty of saying so. Unfashionable. Anachronistic, even.' He looked round meaningfully at the empty chairs. 'You can hardly blame your audience for running away like that. It is the times we live in that are at fault, not they. It's what they call the "climate of opinion" that was hostile, not your hearers personally. Yes, the Zeitgeist is against you.' He paused, and added quietly: 'Or vice versa.'

Joseph nodded. 'Thank you,' he said, touched more by the tone than the words, 'thank you for coming, and thank you for listening. And thank you for what you have just said. Not that I didn't know it already: how tricky it would be to convince them, I mean. I *was* a little taken aback, I must admit, by their lack of politeness, but then that is no concern of mine.'

'Quite, quite, quite,' murmured the priest, getting to his feet and edging through the chairs in Joseph's direction. 'You are a very brave man, you know, Professor Kestler.'

'Brave?' Joseph thought for a moment. 'Yes, I suppose I am,' he allowed, hastening to add, 'but I am not a professor, you must realize. Very far from it. I have no degree, you see, or anything like that.'

The Jesuit made an impatient, buzzing noise: 'No more am I a father, if we want to stick by a very literal use of titles. You are a very learned man, Professor Kestler, and a very courageous one. A twentieth-century cabalist – quite a feat!' He gazed ceiling-wards and went on softly, half to himself: 'It is curious the way Venice has attracted cabalists through the ages. Giorgi lived here – of course you are bound to know that – Bruno was here too, and Agrippa once paid a visit. And then there was the famous Academy of the Urani. Even in quite recent times, I believe, there have been members – or one member at least – of your profession here in Venice. *Un*fortunately,' he added, dipping abruptly downwards as he had when they were introduced and addressing himself, again without warning, to the dog, 'although that is neither here nor there as far as my respect is concerned, you are wrong, wrong, *wrong*. Your theories on cabala, I mean. They are misguided. Whereas, the practice . . .'
He shook his head rapidly from side to side and then rested it for a moment against the puppy's as if to steady it. His earlier embarrassment was evidently coming back to him. 'The actual practice is not only misguided but very wrong indeed. Morally wrong, I mean, in this case. I too have a way with animals, as perhaps you have noticed,' he raised his head towards Joseph and waited for him to agree with this before continuing, 'but I should never allow myself personally to go drawing any conclusions from it. I am good with them, and they do things for me that they wouldn't for other people. It is a gift. A power if you like. But it has nothing to do with magic. How long have you had him?'

'Since yesterday,' said Joseph stiffly. He felt that they were only a hair's breadth away from open disagreement, but was loath to lose the attention of this his only remaining listener.

The priest's colour touched saturation point for the second time that afternoon and he gave Joseph a sharp, quizzical look which quickly changed to one of genuine surprise.

'Then your power is a superior one indeed. Remarkable. Truly remarkable. It puts me in mind of St Francis of Assisi. Now, you wouldn't want to call him a magician, would you?'

Joseph's attention quickened. 'You know, I have never thought of that,' he said interestedly. 'I wonder . . . yes, I wonder now that you come to mention it whether there is any likelihood that St Francis *was* acquainted with cabalist techniques.' And cheering up a little as he went on, he began to examine the question for his listener's benefit; failing, however, to notice the priest's horrified intake of breath as he got more and more into his stride and began to touch on other, related matters. 'Now to take the case of Jesus of Nazareth,' he wound up thoughtfully, 'there we have a grounded possibility that something of the kind did in fact take place: His contacts with the Elders in the Temple and so forth – no shortage of cabalist masters there. You are probably familiar with the theory yourself. But as regards St Francis . . . I wonder . . . I wonder. It's an interesting point you have made there, you realize? Not a new one, of course, seeing that it was one of the standard bugbears of the Inquisition – this business of miracles and magic and so on – but I don't think it has ever been raised in relation to St Francis. Goodness me, yes, the sermon to the birds; the wolf of Gubbio. You have a real point there and no mistake.'

The Jesuit, who had listened to most of this with his face buried in Lapo's fur, had now risen to his feet again, and Joseph could tell from his colour and the way he fidgeted from one foot to the other, flexing slightly at the knees like a goalkeeper, that, despite himself, it was a topic that interested him; in fact, perhaps not only interested him, but shocked and frightened him as well. A long silence followed, which Joseph, for fear of scaring him away altogether, and tardily realizing that he might already have done so, dared not break. At length it was the priest himself who took the initiative. Drawing a deep breath he plunged his hand resolutely into a pocket of his cassock and drew out a wallet covered in black, embroidered felt. From this he extracted a small, creased card, pressed it stealthily into Joseph's hand, and then with a quick backward movement, withdrew it again shamefacedly; continuing, however, to bob up and down in front of him and to proffer little murmurs of abortive explanation. 'I am staying with the monks on San Lazzaro for the rest of the week,' he managed to say haltingly, at last; 'if . . . if you have time at your disposal, you might like to come over and visit me there. There is a most interesting collection of rare manuscripts and things which it might amuse you to browse through. Most, *most* interesting, I would think, for anyone who like yourself is involved . . . is dedicated to this particular field of enquiry.'

Although the suggestion was made taperingly and with the same furtiveness as one contracting with a whore or dope-peddlar (or better still, given the particular bent of the customer, with a simoniac), Joseph hardly noticed, so struck was he of a sudden by the mention of the monks' library and by the promising vistas that it opened. Now there, surely, he thought excitedly, would be the perfect place for his testament – better by far than the University. Why hadn't he thought of it before? If he played his cards right, perhaps the priest would be willing to give him an introduction to the monks there. Perhaps, on the strength of it, the monks might even agree to take the precious manuscript into their charge. In a burst of enthusiasm, he sprang gladly to the invitation; but realized, even as the words left his mouth, that he should have held his eagerness in check. He saw the little priest dither with the card again and stuff it smartly back in his pocket, and could hear in his voice an unmistakable note of regret at having invited him at all as he amended unhappily: 'Well, Professore, I *could* give you my telephone number, of course. But, no . . . No, I think that the best thing would be for *you* to give me *yours*. My being a guest there, you understand.'

He understood, of course – only too well.

'Yes, I understand,' he said, feeling suddenly tired and wishing he was back in his own room again; 'I understand exactly what you mean. I have no number of my own, I'm afraid — but I can be reached at the bar below my pensione. You can get a message to me that way. Just leave a message here,' he extracted a Biro and notebook from the pocket of his overcoat, 'and they will make sure it will reach me. It would be a pleasure to me, Father . . . I am sorry, but I am afraid that I failed to catch your name.'

The priest hesitated again. Then he coughed, hummed, and said thinly: 'Tommaso, Padre Tommaso.' This time his reluctance to commit himself and the aura of illicit assignation that accompanied it were so strong as to be outright offensive; but Joseph merely bowed back at him unruffled, having had his fill of humiliation for the day.

XI

T HE AFTERMATH of the disastrous afternoon at the University was even less painful than Joseph had thought it would be at the time. The numbness wore off gradually, and he was able, as planned, to do a little repair-work to his self-esteem; to add a prop here, a patch there, and make sure it stayed upright long enough to see his testament to completion. For until that was done, he couldn't afford to crumble: neither morally, nor physically.

Since the evening that he had seen the surgeon and had learnt from what he had not been told how ill he really was, it had been the prospect of his work, of course, and in particular the prospect of handing it over to the University for safe-keeping, that had done the necessary buttressing for him on the material plane. That thought, that hope, the preparations and sheer mental commitment it had involved, had kept his body going. Yet now that this stay had been so abruptly removed, instead of the collapse that might have been expected, the terms of his dependency merely seemed to have shifted round a little. Now he was no longer alive on account of his work, but was working on account of the fact that he was alive. There were other, different things to do, besides. There were the details of Lapo's care to be discussed with Emilio. (This afternoon, for example, here they were together, taking him down to the gardens of the Biennale, so that he could make contact with a healthy expanse of grass instead of the usual paving-stones. Emilio had stressed the importance of making canine contacts also, in order to give the puppy a sense of specific identity; but to Joseph's way of thinking this was hardly necessary since Lapo seemed to have a fairly strong one already.) There were the meals to be prepared. There was Emilio to chat to on unrelated matters, and Emilio to be silent with, as in fact both of them more often than not preferred. These were the things that now buoyed him up, and comforted him to the point of being able to continue his work. It was amazing, the frailty and yet the resilience of this mutually supporting structure, he thought as he glanced with affection at these two late-won friends of his, walking – one high, one low – on either side. By rights he should now be dead, and his uncompleted work should be smouldering, along with his other unclaimed belongings, on the municipal rubbish dump; yet here they still were – body and testament – leaning up against each other and deriving from each other a force that neither singularly possessed, like a couple of precariously balanced playing cards.

Well, another day or two of equilibrium and the testament would be finished; although quite what he would do with it once it was, he had still not decided. If Trevisan did not get in touch with him – if his desertion, that is, proved as final as it seemed – and if the priest did not telephone, then as a last resort he supposed he would now have to run the risk of handing it over to Emilio upon completion. In fact, he had recently begun thinking that from the point of view of trustworthiness he might do a lot worse. He smiled fondly at the untidy figure shambling along beside him, and noted the tact with which its pace had slowed to match his own: Emilio was not clever, of course, and he was not discerning and he was most definitely not interested in the occult, his mind being filled with an odd mixture of ideas which he seemed to pick up and stock there on the strength of their supposed modernity alone; but he was (to use one of the old-fashioned concepts that he himself would have no use for) a good man. He was nice, and kind, and helpful, and the friendship that he offered was spontaneous and genuine. More than could be said for Trevisan, alas. In his favour also was the fact that his graduation thesis (on which, in time to the mysteriously lenient rhythms of the Italian university, he had been engaged for six years) concerned amongst other things the church of San Francesco della Vigna, the architecture of which had been inspired by Giorgi's magic. This made a connecting link of sorts, and encouraged Joseph to think that he might find his own work not only acceptable, but interesting, and maybe even helpful. (It was not that he was given to boasting, but just that he knew that a student of any place or age would be hard put to find a better authority on Giorgi's number mystique.) Unfortunately, he did seem to remember that the one time they had touched on the topic, Emilio had dismissed the magical element laughingly as a 'load of rubbish'; but there again, this attitude of his (touched as it had been with humour), was perhaps less uncompromising than Trevisan's and perhaps safer in the long run than the priest's. Apart from the factor of interest, which might or might not be present, the testament would never anger Emilio, and never frighten him either. Yes, all things considered, choice and necessity might go together for once in a while, and he might in the end turn out to be the safest depositary of all.

They had now reached the gardens, and as they shuffled along companionably through the carpet of fallen leaves, their silence enlivened by the slushing of their steps and by the occasional hoot of a passing ship, the moment seemed so favourable to Joseph and the need to unburden himself so strong that he found himself more than once on the very point of clearing his throat and preparing to speak; but still he hesitated. For the matter of the testament was not all there was to it: there was also the suspended question of the Catcher to be dealt with.

Shortly after Lapo's arrival, he had sent one chilling message – a slip of cardboard pushed under the bedroom door, on which was scrawled the drawing of a dog, and underneath it the traditional caption: 'Attenti al cane' – beware of the dog. A message which, knowing the sender's habits as he did, and noticing that the drawing seemed to be of a very lifeless sort of dog, Joseph had taken to mean a less traditional and much more menacing: 'Beware for the dog's sake.' He had not shown it to Emilio yet though – since unless you knew about the Catcher it was harmless enough to be passed off as a bland form of teasing — but had merely stressed to him once again the importance of keeping Lapo on his lead when in the neighbourhood.

This had been followed by a stretch of quiet, which worried Joseph almost more than any action to date. It was days since he had seen the Catcher leave his room now, and, stare as he might at the shadowy figure behind the blinds, there was no way of telling what he was up to. The only certainty was that he was up to *something*, and something that threatened Joseph more closely and more painfully than ever before. Twice he had seen the Catcher sharpening what had looked to be his hook on the window-ledge; twice, or maybe more, he had thought he heard the light patter of footsteps echoing his own as he made his way homewards through the narrow alleys that led to the pensione; but of neither fact was he really sure. That was the trouble with the Catcher: you could never pin him down. He left no traces behind him, and no tangible proofs. Even his schoolfellows, whom Joseph — rashly as it had turned out — had questioned about him, seemed anxious to keep up this aura of secrecy. They had answered none of Joseph's questions and volunteered no information, but had stared blankly back at him, one of them tapping mockingly at the side of his head as if to signal to his companions that the insistent old man had best be treated as a lunatic, and another back-stepping from the group and reappearing in the company of a janitor who had eyed Joseph suspiciously and had shooed him away with an angry wave of the hand. Wouldn't it be better to tell Emilio something of all this as well, he wondered? Show him the message? Explain about the cats, and the reason for keeping Lapo away from the palazzo? From a tactical point of view it would certainly seem that he should. But, then again, if he did — if he told him straight out and in so many words that not only was he a magician with a perilous secret to hand on, but was also being persecuted on the side by a schoolchild-cum-demon who was threatening to injure Lapo — would Emilio, even if he wanted to, be able to believe him? Or would he just humour him and classify his confession privately as another load of rubbish? It certainly did not sound a very

99

convincing tale. A similar disclosure – and only a partial one, at that – had already cost him Trevisan's friendship; so was it wise to jeopardize this last remaining one which was dearer to him still? It would be terrible if Emilio too should mock him, or misunderstand, for he very much doubted he could bear yet another failure, yet another breach.

While he had been thinking, without noticing it Joseph had been opening his mouth and then shutting it, and coughing, and clearing his throat with regular frequency. Each time he did so, Emilio would give a polite, sideward glance and a fleeting smile, but did not venture to disturb him, except by nudging him now and again to draw his attention to some particularly amusing antic of Lapo's. Although there were no recent signs of the dogs Emilio had wanted him to meet, the puppy seemed truly and rewardingly in his element. He scampered ahead of his owners, churning up the leaves as he went and snapping at them delightedly as they fluttered downwards, worrying at them, chasing them, and treating them much as if they were a more available sort of pigeon. Now and then he would whisk round on himself so abruptly as to lose his balance, and after his first indignant surprise at being upside-down, would slither along on his side for a stretch, wriggling an ecstatic path through the carpet of leaves. Joseph watched him tenderly, his heart full of misgivings, still wretchedly undecided as to how much to tell Emilio, or whether to tell him anything at all. Which did he most wish to protect, anyway, he asked himself impatiently, exasperated by his own dithering? The testament? That went without saying. But the puppy too? *And* the friendship? And wouldn't silence protect all three, as long as he kept his eyes well open?

As things turned out, he was wrong about this and less than an hour later had occasion to regret his decision, although what he in fact regretted – and bitterly – was not the silence itself, which proved ultimately wise, but the fact that he had not backed it by the vigilant watch he had intended.

Quite how and why this came about, he could not remember clearly afterwards. He had been tired by the long walk – that for sure – and he had unthinkingly accepted Emilio's suggestion that he take a vaporetto instead of walking back along the waterfront of Riva degli Schiavoni as they had come. It seemed a perfectly sound idea and a welcome one. Equally sound and straightforward had seemed that Emilio himself walk the distance with Lapo. There was a charge made for dogs as for normal passengers; besides which, there was not much amusement value in a boat as far as Lapo was concerned. So, as the dog trotted off happily at Emilio's side, Joseph plumped himself down on the bench of the imbarcadero to wait for the next boat, and watched their two disappearing figures without the least foreshadowing of danger.

The boat was a long time coming. At St Mark's he had to change and wait some time for a second, and when it arrived it turned out to be one of the big, slow ones that stopped off at each point of embarkation along the route, nosing their way in a leisurely zigzag fashion from one bank to the other. He was mildly surprised, therefore, when he finally got to his own stop to find that there was no Emilio to meet him, and no Lapo; but without giving much thought to the matter, he merely shrugged his shoulders and began to make his way back to his lodgings. The afternoon had been well spent, but there was still a certain amount of work to be done over the testament, and he could not afford to spend any of the precious evening hours in waiting around for his friends' return. They might have gone straight back there themselves, anyway, he reasoned; or Emilio might have met up with a fellow student, or taken a longer route. There were any number of explanations for their delay, and no cause for worry at this stage.

As he turned into the alley, he was relieved to see that Emilio, as he had expected, was back already. He was standing by the entrance, one hand in his pocket, and the other shading his eyes as he scanned the narrow passageway in both directions. When he saw Joseph, however, he gave a jump and a very half-hearted wave and hastened towards him, his spikes of hair quivering as he ran; the empty lead dangling at his side making Joseph realize instantly, and with a thud of recognition in his chest as if the moment was one that he had already lived through and one that had already cost him pain, that Lapo was missing.

Despite his haste, Emilio was apologetic but calm: 'He slipped his collar, Joe. Fancy that. I reckoned he must have heard you coming. Didn't you see him anywhere? He's only just this minute gone – he can't be far.' And he began whistling for him, and called out the dog's name a couple of times.

Joseph, whose face had meanwhile gone a greyish colour and had become strangely set in its expression, groped for the wall behind him, and propped his elbow against it to prevent himself from falling, telling himself in a dull kind of fury that he would do better to beat his head against it instead. For how *could* he have been so negligent and foolish? Not only had he told Emilio nothing openly and explained nothing, but with crass stupidity – minutes, seconds even, after thinking things out so carefully – he had slackened his own vigilance, and had let the pair of them saunter off alone like that, without even giving him a hint. How could he have been so remiss?

'Mi 'spiace, Joe,' Emilio was now saying, beginning to look a little worried now that he saw the clay-like pallor of Joseph's face. 'I'm sorry, I really am. But there's no need to take it so hard. He'll be back again soon. He won't run away. He knows his home is with us now. I'm sorry it should have happened, but it wasn't my fault. The collar must have been loose, and he just pulled it over his ears and ran off. But he'll be back all right. He can't have gone far.'

With an effort, Joseph levered his elbow against the wall and stood straight again. He had scarcely listened to what Emilio had been saying, but the last remark struck him as a sensible one all the same: he was right, Lapo could not be far away. And although this fact was not much comfort in itself (in fact the closer he was, the greater was the danger), it definitely meant that there might still be a chance of saving him. He gave his head a good shake, and placing a forgiving hand on Emilio's arm, whispered slowly but urgently: 'Right, then. We will make a thorough search of the district. You will go down towards the bar and comb all the nearest streets on this side. I will cross over the bridge further down and see if by any chance he has gone over to the square. We will meet back here in quarter of an hour. If you find him, give me a whistle and I will understand. I don't think I can manage a whistle myself – my mouth is too dry – but I'll call out to you if I am the one that finds him.'

It was in fact Joseph who found him. He saw him as soon as he emerged from the dark burrow of the sottoportego (a narrow, overhung passage, this, cut through the foundations of the corner building to give public access to the square on the canal side) and into the pale, late afternoon greyness of the open space beyond. The square was empty, the windows of the shops were not yet lit, and the only objects of any brightness were the fruits of the persimmon tree which hung vulnerably on its leafless branches like little orange dots of colour on a dull, wintry canvas. Lapo was on the far side of the square, directly beneath the Catcher's window. The window was open, and from behind a partially thrown-back shutter a small, thin arm could be seen, making a funny jerking movement. The puppy appeared to be watching some object on the ground in front of him, his whiskered, seal-like head cocked to one side, and was crouched playfully with extended forepaws as if preparing to leap.

Joseph, calmer and more level-headed than he had ever imagined himself capable of being in such an extreme situation – a situation where every hundredth of a second had its weight and could prove decisive – lost not a whit of time or self-possession. He shut his eyes tightly, plunged into deep concentration, and in a voice that startled him by its force and authority, called out Lapo's number. The effect was instantaneous. As during the demonstration at the University, the dog stiffened to rigidity, as if he had been suddenly coated by an invisible mantle of starch, paused in the very act of pouncing on the lump of meat that dangled before his nose, and then, like a toy that has been pushed aside, rocked forwards and toppled to the ground.

Joseph crossed the square with awkwardly hurried steps, intent upon nothing but the next stage of rescue. With as much delicacy as if it had been a priceless porcelain statue, he bent and picked up the stiff little form and laid his ear against the rib-cage, finding to his relief that, although he had had to act without taking any precautions this time, the heart was beating regularly. Then, still very carefully, he whispered more words and numbers into the ear, lifting it like the lid of a box to obtain better acoustics. Not until the puppy had relaxed to something like the normal tension, though, and he had fastened the belt of his mackintosh firmly about the neck, did he spare attention for the rest of the scene and the other actor in it.

The Catcher was leaning boldly out of the window now, not just his arm but his head and shoulders in full view, looking down at Joseph with a wide smile across his face. In his hand he still held the thin, insidious nylon thread that was attached to the bait. Joseph bent down to examine it more closely, placing his foot firmly over the piece of meat to prevent its withdrawal. He frowned: it was a simple, fresh-smelling square of lean meat – it looked as if it might even be steak – tied by a loose knot to the line itself. There was no hook in the meat and, as far as he could make out, no poison. Nor did it appear to have been devised as a taunt, for it was clear that the meat would have shortly fallen from the thread of its own accord. He undid the knot and put the meat in his pocket where Lapo, who had started squirming in his arms with reawakened interest, could not get at it. Then, still cradling the puppy fast to him, he took a deep breath and looked straight up above him at his enemy's face.

Any puzzlement he had felt over the reason for this strangely innocuous hoax – this trap within a trap, that wasn't a trap at all – left him the instant he saw the Catcher's expression. It was one of triumph: arrogant and absolute triumph. The Catcher had won, or so it seemed, a decisive victory. Seeing him there, framed by the darkened window, the whites of his eyes and the glinting metal teeth highlighted by the surrounding shadow and forming a small, brilliant triangle that shone down at him with amused and total satisfaction, Joseph had no puzzlement either over the reason for his triumph. It was indeed so simple that the only wonder was that he had not thought of it before. The reason for it was, of course, that he had forced Joseph into disclosing his power to him – into openly demonstrating his magicianhood.

The realization, and what it implied, hit Joseph with the force of a bullet, making him stagger backwards under its impact. So this, he thought to himself panic-stricken, as he held Lapo tightly to him and braced himself to withstand the taunting gaze from above – this was what he had been after all along. The Catcher was not, as he had artlessly supposed until now, a separate problem at all. The Catcher was connected to the magic. The Catcher was after his magic. Through these long months of careful persecution, he had been leading him – patiently and inexorably goading him – into revealing his magician's power. As he had always vaguely suspected but never fully understood, it was an instrumental cruelty he had been using. The cats had been nothing to him. Lapo had meant nothing. They had been mere means by which to arrive at his goal. How neat it all was, thought Joseph bitterly. How cunning. How simple. And how foolish of him not to have realized this earlier on. Had he been able to summon one, he would almost have liked to return the enemy's smile to show his appreciation of the way he had managed things. Talent – of whatever kind – should never go unrecognized. A little irony might have helped him cover up his foolishness, too.

No smile came, but he stood his ground unflinchingly all the same, comforted to some extent by the fact that however naked he might now appear in his enemy's eyes, having dropped his camouflage and allowed himself to be seen in the very act of practising his magic, he was not the only one to have made a revelation. In this respect they were on a level now. The Catcher knew who he was, but he too knew who the Catcher was. Or what he was. He stared calmly back into the sharp, mocking countenance, looking for some sign of weakness or hesitancy. But the mask was impenetrable. A waxwork again, only a smiling one. Viewed impartially, he supposed, the expression that it wore might still be taken as that of a teasing child; but viewed as he now viewed it, with the knowledge of what lay behind it, not even the addition of a pair of horns or pointed ears would have served to make things clearer to him. Whatever reluctance he might have felt in the past over accepting such beings, however fanciful some of his predecessors' theories about evil agents had always seemed to him and however ridiculous, he now knew beyond a doubt (yes, *knew*, for he was able to see and hear and touch the object, and what is this if not to know?) that what he was faced with was not a mere child at all, but a veritable power of evil.

He was staring at an agent of evil, and it was staring back. How long it was necessary to go on staring, he did not know. He only felt instinctively that he must not be the first to drop his gaze. Lapo whined with impatience in his arms, and he bent to set him on the ground beside him without lowering his eyes from the Catcher's, keeping a close hold of the improvised lead. As he did so, however, the Catcher, who appeared to attach less importance to the staring contest, gave a scornful little wave, dropped the thread he had been holding, and, leaving Joseph with the vaguely cheated feeling of a theatre-goer on whom the curtain has been dropped in mid-drama, banged the shutters to.

For some moments he went on staring foolishly at the slatted wooden surface of the shutters, but then, more from anticlimax than relief, he felt his muscles slowly relax, and fishing into his pocket he removed the lump of meat and threw it aside, well out of Lapo's reach. There was no use carrying it around with him, for the question of its analysis had become futile. The Catcher was not after Lapo, as he had never been after the cats, in anything but a purely contingent way. He had been after the magic. And now that he had tracked it down, it would, of course, be the testament, and not Lapo, that would need the greater protection; for that was presumably what he would be after next.

Not that Lapo would be entirely safe either, though, he reminded himself warily, and not that the Catcher might not still find use for his cruelty. He might try kidnapping the dog, for example, and bartering its safety for the manuscript – sending Lapo's ears, tail, etc., etc., back to his master one by one until he capitulated and paid the ransom. A trick like that would be very much in his style. Or else he might switch his attention to Emilio, and try to get at him that way – through his friend.

In fact, there were so many terrible things that he might do, that Joseph couldn't help feeling a sudden urge to hand over the testament to him straight away before he could get round to doing any of them; but when he realized the enormity of what he was thinking, he chased the idea away, shocked by his own weakness. He must never think a thing like that. Goodness, no. It would be the end of everything. He mustn't hand over anything, or give up anything, and he must let no harm come to his friends. There must be no weakness and no wavering. He must fight it out in person, alone.

The first thing to do – the first obvious and sensible thing – was to finish the testament as soon as possible, and until it was finished to keep it with him every second of the day and night. This went for Lapo too. He couldn't really hope to watch over Emilio in the same way, but then Emilio was probably safer as he was: knowing nothing, and left out of the proceedings altogether. Then, as soon as the testament was ready, he must take it away and hide it in some sufficiently safe and remote place without the Catcher's knowledge (and even without Padre What's-it's help he thought that the island might still be his best bet), and sit tight to the very end, trying as best he could to throw him off the scent.

He had made a mistake in revealing himself, but then so had the enemy. He knew what he was up against now, and he knew why. The testament was as yet undiscovered (perhaps – although he thought it unlikely – the Catcher did not yet know of its existence) and he had still some means at his disposal to see that it remained so. Added to which – extreme evils calling for extreme remedies – he still had the resource of the safety device to fall back on. Now that he had faced his enemy openly and seen him for what he was, the classic solution no longer seemed as ruthless to him as it had before. No more ruthless than the Catcher, anyway. It was expressly against such ills that it had been devised. He would waste no more time, and have no more scruples about it, but would finish the text and insert the necessary passage that very evening.

XII

S O AS NOT to miss any of the trickier parts of the story, it is perhaps a good idea to take another outside look at Joseph Kestler, the magician, as he lives out one of the last peaceful evenings of his difficult life.

He and Emilio, having taken Lapo along with them and having moored him securely to the leg of a chair, are having supper together. Their shared relief at having found him again (for some of Joseph's anxiety has brushed itself off on to Emilio as well, although he still doesn't know the reason for it) has brought them very close to one another – closer than they have ever been before or will have occasion to be again. They have chosen a small, secluded restaurant on the Zattere – the long stretch of quayside opposite the island of the Giudecca – and a table facing seawards from which they can watch the passage of the boats.

Conversation between them neither flags nor flows, but now and again Emilio makes some comment on the food, or the pensione, or the progress he is making with his basset horn, or things like that, which Joseph answers with the odd, absent-minded murmur. It is worth noticing (Joseph has noticed it, for one, and is grateful for it) that Emilio has quite given up trying to benefit from Joseph's English. Nowadays, with Lapo as their common interest, what little talking they do is nearly always in Italian. This is presumably due to the fact that Lapo himself is such a very Italian dog.

During one of their long, easy silences, of which there are many, Joseph takes a tentacle of squid from his plate and dangles it in front of Lapo's nose. It disappears in a trice and Emilio, who is paying for the dinner, looks on very good-naturedly as the dog cleans his muzzle with his tongue and waits for more. Joseph watches Emilio as he watches Lapo watching the plate. It is not easy to tell what he is thinking, but he looks a little pleased and a little cross at the same time, and it may well be that he is thinking over to himself for at least the second time – if not the third or the fourth – what a good, kind personality he has come across in this unexpected quarter. He may also be kicking himself for not having recognized these qualities earlier on, when there would have been time for him to make use of them: thinking that if he had gone about things in the right way he could have won Emilio over to his side, remembering how impressed he was when he lulled the dog to sleep for him by whispering its number, and regretting having sought the insensitive ears of the University professors instead of concentrating on the far more sympathetic pair that have been in all senses much closer to him all the time.

Yes, I think this must be it. He has made another tardy recognition; only this time, instead of an enemy, he has recognized what might have turned out to be excellent human material to be coached as his successor. But now, of course, it is too late for anything like that. There are too many preliminaries to be gone through, too much to teach him, too much that needs explaining. He hasn't the energy now for such an undertaking, nor the time, nor even the courage. And anyway, now that he knows what he is up against, he is secretly rather glad for Emilio's sake that the battle is to be fought in single combat. The priest has not telephoned: that is as expected. Trevisan has failed him: that he had not expected but he has learned to accept. The University is a closed and painful chapter that is best forgotten. No, all he can do now is to insert the fateful safety device (and with that inserted there is yet *another* good reason for keeping the testament well away from the hands of a nice, uncomplicated man like Emilio), marshal his energies and, while he still has a little strength and dexterity left, smuggle the testament over to the island of San Lazzaro on his own account and hide it among the volumes in the library there when no one is looking. It is a desperate enough solution – weak, hasty and ill-planned – but there seems at this late stage to be no alternative.

While Joseph has been mulling over these or similar things in his mind, the waiter has cleared the table, and has now lit a stub of candle and brought over two fresh glasses and a bottle of liqueur which Emilio has begun to pour out for them. Joseph holds out thumb and finger to indicate a very small amount for himself. Emilio smiles again: 'Take care of yourself, Joe,' he says with a friendly note of warning in his voice. 'Are you sure that doctor of yours knows what he is about? I know it's none of my business, but there's a very good hospital in Padua. It might be an idea for you to go over there for a check-up. There's no boat-service running at this time of year, but I could borrow a car off a friend and take you there myself, if you like.'

Joseph swallows, a little taken aback: he is not used to people offering to do things for him. 'Thank you, Emilio,' he whispers, almost inaudibly, 'but you have done enough already. More than enough. It has taken us a long time to get to know each other, but that was no fault of yours. You found Lapo for me when I needed him; you helped me take care of him; and here you are taking me out and giving me . . .' he slipped Lapo another tentacle, and gave a guilty smile, 'giving *us* this delicious dinner. No, I can't have you going to any more trouble on my account.' Here he stops and looks down at the table, evidently thinking hard. 'Unless,' he adds slowly, 'unless . . . yes, there *is* one thing, come to think of it. Tomorrow morning I have a little job to do, and I may have to leave rather early. If you could keep an eye on Lapo for me till I get back, I'd be very grateful. Yes. It would take a load off my mind: to know that while I am gone, and if . . . if I'm late or anything should happen to me, you will be there to look after him.'

A melancholy little speech, this, if you read it rightly, and a melancholy scene: the passing ships, the candlelight, the dog, and the two chronically lonely men, united by a tenuous thread of understanding which – as is often the case with interhuman bridges, and nearly always so when one of the parties is dedicated to a cause – can hold only as long as they put no weight on it. That they are both, in varying degrees, aware of this makes it even sadder in a way, but Joseph, for one, should not be surprised at it, seeing that for the sake of his work he has opted from the very start for solitude and secrecy and silence.

Whatever doubt we may ourselves have as to the importance of this work of his, and as to whether it has been worth the sacrifice, one thing is certain: from the administrative angle at least he has so far muffed things badly. He is, or thinks he is, the bearer of a vitally important message to humanity. The official custodians of science are not interested in the message and will neither take it in nor pass it on. (This is a sweeping conclusion to draw, of course, from one rebuff at the hands of a small group of scholars from a small, provincial university, and it could be argued that Joseph has taken the snub too much to heart and that he ought to hawk his wares around a little more brazenly, and try elsewhere, and again, and again; especially if he is so persuaded as to their value. But, apart from the fact that there is not much time left for marketing, the conclusion is basically a sound one, I suppose, and one he could have drawn – and probably did in his heart of hearts – the moment he embarked on his career.) Whereas he himself, with his strict and rather conventional standards of what is best from an intellectual point of view, mistrusts any unofficial or semi-official custodians. The borderline of the scientific world, the shadier, hazier areas where theory and proof rub shoulders and scratch each other's backs in a more friendly and accommodating fashion, is not for him. He wants to put his work not on the borderline but in the centre. In the temple. On the high altar itself. Or wanted to, that is; but realizing that he can't – not for the time being anyway – what he now wants to do is to hide his message away somewhere where it can hibernate in safety and await the more promising climate of a new and different scientific springtime.

The idea is not a bad one in itself – in fact, it is hard to think of a better one under the circumstances – but the weakness in it is that Joseph has left it very late for putting it into practice. With all the stress he has gone through lately, his mind has lost some of its grip (witness, for example, his worsening relationship with the boy who lives across the way; witness what weird ideas he comes up with when trying to analyse it) and it is clear that his bodily health too is declining rapidly. Emilio has noticed this; Joseph himself has noticed it; and from the detached position we are now in, we too can notice it with a shade more realism than they. His coughing is weaker and quieter, but it has a dry, metallic ring to it, and breaks out more often. His hands are a little shaky, his appetite has gone, and every movement seems to cost him effort. His recent set-to in the square with his minute enemy (or with the perhaps relatively innocuous child whom he has cast in this role) seems to have taken a great deal out of him, he appears to have aged and become greyer, more drawn and more wrinkled than he was, not only at the start of the story but at the start of the day.

It would be wrong, though, to think that he is beaten yet. For we must remember – however difficult it may be to do so seriously – that he has as strong a motive to drive him as any human being is likely to have. He is driven, that is, by moral necessity. He has a discovery to impart of revolutionary potential. He has his testament to save.

When he and Emilio return to their lodgings, it is easy to see that the testament is uppermost in his mind. Lapo, bounding ahead of them up the staircase, stops in front of the door to Joseph's bedroom, sniffs at the crack and gives a soft but unmistakable growl; and this fact – a fact that the normal dog-owner would find a little odd maybe, but nothing more serious than that – is enough to throw Joseph into a state of considerable alarm. One hand on the scruff of the dog's neck, he places his precious bundle of papers on the floor and clamps a foot over them so as not to leave them unguarded for a single instant, and with the other hand tests the lock to see if it has been tampered with. Then he turns the key softly, listens for a moment at the doorway, throws open the door with a crash, and tumbles over the threshold in a tangle of dog, leash and manuscript. Watched by a baffled Emilio he lurches over to his writing-desk and begins thumbing urgently through his papers, counting them over and over to check that none are missing. Having done this, he takes to prowling round the room, his eyes scanning the floor, the shelves and the bed itself. Next he tests the bathroom, and finally, apparently still not satisfied, the latch of the window. He is evidently deeply worried.

Emilio, no doubt thinking that his friend has been the victim of a chance pilferer, or else that he is merely being – the way some elderly people are – a little over-cautious about his few, valueless belongings, gives him a hand in the search and has a look under the bed and in the cupboard, but he doesn't seem to take the matter very seriously and when he has checked things to his own satisfaction, he says goodnight and takes Lapo off with him to his own room.

Joseph himself is clearly still unconvinced, though, and as soon as the door is closed he goes back to his investigations with redoubled energy, concentrating in particular on the area around his desk. When he has finished, he stands looking at it thoughtfully for a long while, shutting and opening his eyes by turns as if comparing the present layout with some image in his memory. Then he bites on a nail and heaves an angry sigh. Presumably he is regretting his first impulsive scanning of the papers which has now made it difficult to tell what meddling, if any, has taken place during his absence.

His next move, surprisingly enough, is to go and fetch Lapo back from Emilio's room, and it is interesting to note that he has quite some difficulty over this: not over persuading him to leave Emilio, so much as over persuading him to enter his own bedroom. Eventually he has actually to drag him across the threshold; and once inside, the dog crouches down close to the exit and goes in for a long bout of sniffing and whimpering before settling down to sleep – behaviour which, naturally, does nothing to steady Joseph's nerves. He goes back to his papers, in fact, with something like frenzy now, and looking uncannily like a dog himself, even goes so far as to put his nose to them and inhale. This makes him sneeze violently, but before the sneezing a grimace of disgust crosses his features, his hands start to tremble, and from the topmost sheet of paper he removes an invisible wisp of something – presumably a hair or a piece of thread – and holds it against the light to examine it, his hands no longer trembling but actually shaking.

The cause of these sharp, jerky tremors (so sharp that what with them and the sneeze, he eventually loses hold of whatever it was he had found, and is unable to find it again) would seem, however, from the look of things, to be anger rather than fear. With what is unmistakably a grunt of impatience, he turns back the frayed cuffs of his shirt, rolls them determinedly to elbow level, seats himself at his desk with such force that the air-cushion bounces beneath him, as if saying to himself or to some unseen adversary in a crabby fashion: 'Well, here we are then: you have asked for it, and I shall see to it that you get it!', and begins to write.

He writes, as in his best and most inspired moments, fast and firmly. There is no more trembling, no head-scratching, and no hesitation. His hand scarcely leaves the paper. Once he half rises to draw down a book from the shelf above and consults its index rapidly, searching for a name, maybe, or checking the spelling of one he already knows. Twice he pounces on a cigarette and scratches a minute, wax-coated match against the matchbox, but unable to spare the attention that is needed to light it, pushes all smoking utensils irritably aside each time and returns to his work. The whole process takes him little short of four and a half hours.

When he is through, he has a go at rereading what he has written, but the business appears too distasteful to him, and he gives up after the first few lines and shakes his head repeatedly with a look of defeat. After placing the pages he has written in a large blue folder, already bulky with manuscript, and tying the tapes firmly around it, he lies down on the bed, fully dressed except for his shoes, and stuffs the folder under the pillow, and the pillow firmly under his head.

Despite the position of his body, though, stretched out neatly and symmetrically in apparent relaxation, it is easy to tell that he is not asleep. He is stirred every now and then by a light twitch at the hands and the knees. His eyes are closed, but again, every so often, the lids flutter and open imperceptibly and ripple as the eyeball passes from side to side. No, he is not sleeping, nor even resting: he is on the watch.

Poor Joseph: tired, ill, his success unrecognized – except by one small being whose recognition constitutes a threat. The strain of being a magician in the year 1982 would appear to have almost worn him out. And his task is not yet anything like completed.

XIII

JOSEPH woke up with a jump and a guilty feeling at having let himself fall asleep at all, and turning his head sideways on the pillow he felt for the reassuring hardness of the folder beneath before dragging himself into a sitting position. Lapo was still sleeping, but he was curled tight against the door with his nose pressed wedge-like to the crack, and the fact that he had presumably kept up his uncomfortable position all night worried Joseph all the more. Dogs, he well knew, were sensitive to atmosphere. It was clear that Lapo found the room as oppressive as he did himself, and clear therefore that his fears on the evening before had been well-grounded: lock or no lock, shutters or no shutters, the Catcher had been there – had penetrated right into the intimacy of his bedroom. He had not found what he was after, to be sure, for the testament had never left Joseph's side all evening (except during dinner, when he had sat on it instead), but from the papers that had been left lying on the desk he must have cottoned on to the fact of its existence and whereabouts, and it was, Joseph knew, only a matter of time before he struck again and made a bolder bid for it.

Slowly but with great deliberation, he hoisted himself out of bed and crossed over to the window. Through the slats of the shutters, which he left prudently drawn, he could see just enough of the outside world to tell that it was early and raining. And so much the better, he thought to himself with a stern nod of the head: the less he could see of the Catcher, the less the Catcher could see of him.

Lapo, awakened by Joseph's movements and no doubt sensing his departure, lifted his nose from the fissure of the doorway and eyed his master questioningly, watching intently as, with rapid gestures and a deftness that the urgency of the situation seemed to have resuscitated in him despite his weakness, Joseph girded himself to carry out the last lap of his plan for the saving of the manuscript.

Taking it from its hiding-place under the pillow, he first wrapped the folder carefully in sheet after sheet of newspaper, then trussed the resulting package with string and popped it in a plastic bag, and then repeated the whole procedure three times over before firmly taping the outmost bag – a white one – with various criss-crossing bands of blue adhesive tape. This done, still leaving the shutters firmly closed, he padded quietly towards the bathroom to prepare himself, performing his washing and dressing in almost total darkness, and keeping the communicating door to the bedroom purposefully ajar and the plastic-covered bundle balanced on the corner of the washbasin.

So it had come to this, he thought sadly, as he pulled on his clothes, donned his faithful mackintosh and tiptoed softly down the passage to leave Lapo in the custody of Emilio: in order to effect this last desperate ruse for the protection of his papers, here he was, sneaking out of his lodgings in the dark hours of the early morning, a parcel stuffed furtively under his arm and a heavy, guilty feeling inside him, for anything as if instead of trying to escape one, he were himself a thief. And in true burglar style, he inched open the door to his friend's room, just wide enough to admit the puppy, drew it slowly to again without waking Emilio, who was snoring peacefully on his back, looking somewhat like a large puppy himself, and crept stealthily down the staircase and across the stained marble flagstones of the hall.

Once outside, he gave a quick glance around him, hunched his shoulders briskly as if to pull them closer together, and still on tiptoe but moving faster and more nimbly, left the cover of the doorway and began to make his way down the deserted alley towards the wider thoroughfare that led to the imbarcadero.

Half-way along he paused to look behind him and make sure he was not being followed. The alley was still clear. Nothing stirred; nothing disturbed the stillness of the early morning air, except the gentle, slanting current of the rain and the swaying of a line of neglected washing that hung forlornly dripping from a window nearby. Unless . . . unless . . . wait a minute . . . He paused again; he was not sure of this, but at the very far end, when he trained his eyes properly and concentrated hard on the patterns of light and darkness, he thought he could just make out a suspect patch of shadow that fell like a small, dusky column across the paving – a shadow the length and breadth of a child's, with a dark, thick, turbid quality about it. And unless he was mistaken, it too was moving.

On rounding the corner he paused again and pressed himself well back against the wall to listen for eventual footfalls, sure that for all the patter of the rain and the drumming of his heart he would recognize them if he heard them, and waited there, splayed like a sole against the moist surface of the bricks, until he had counted to one hundred and forty-four (which, as twice seventy-two, was one of the strongest numbers he could think of, of a suitably wieldly dimension). But no sound came.

Cautiously, his head wobbling with the strain like an aged tortoise's, he craned it round the edge of the building and glanced once more down the alleyway. The column was no longer to be seen, but now – far more worrying than any shadow, and far more substantial – a strange, black, bulky shape was moving centrally down the narrow passage, making fast in his direction. He drew back in alarm and flattened himself against the wall again, debating feverishly whether he should wait until he had identified the shape or plough ahead, regardless of its identity, and keep what lead he had on it. Then, summoning courage and stifling a cough, he risked a second glance, to recognize with a feeling of immense relief, no threatening, dark monster at all, but the figure of an errand-boy trundling before him a huge basketful of bread and shielding both his head and the basket from the rain by a black plastic refuse bag.

With a half-hearted smile at his own foolishness and a

somewhat vexed mutter to himself that there were dangers enough to contend with without adding imaginary ones, Joseph squared his shoulders purposefully once more, stepped into the open, and headed towards the Grand Canal. There had been little time for strategy, but as a minimal measure he had decided not to take a boat directly to the Lido and thence to San Lazzaro – the Lido boats being more crowded, even at this time of the morning – but to stop off instead at the island of San Giorgio; tack back again to the city; and undertake the main part of his journey from there.

Even as he resumed his walk, though, running diligently through the details again so as to be able to act fast and smoothly no matter what stress he might be under at the time, from the corner of his eye he saw the small fleeting shadow of earlier emerge from the street behind and disappear into a doorway, and it occurred to him that his first impression had most likely been correct: the Catcher might well be following after all. But he noted the fact more calmly this time – his alarm seeming to have spent itself over the episode of the errand-boy – and merely tried in a fairly mechanical way to quicken his pace.

The effort was too great for him to keep it up for long, but as he went back – a little out of breath – to his usual speed and forged steadily on, he thought that it might in any case be better for him to go slowly, so as not to approach the imbarcadero until just before the boat got in. Like that, he could be sure of being amongst the last in boarding, and it would be easier to see whether or not the child had followed him aboard. And if he had, then he could change his mind at the last minute, dodge him, and wait for a second boat.

As he neared the raft, keeping a watchful eye on the water traffic so as not to miss the arrival of the next vaporetto, he became surer and surer of the Catcher's presence. Not only was he tailing him, he felt, but was doing so at particularly close range. He had always been able to sense the child from the feeling of dankness that went with him: it had coated his hands when he had touched him; his papers had smelt of it the evening before; his room had still reeked of it this morning. And now at intervals depending on the wind he could smell it so strongly that it made him cough. What was more, he could distinctly hear those irregular little footsteps of his tagging along behind, and without turning round but just by squinting sideways could catch clearer and clearer glimpses of the unmistakable shadowy patch, either standing deceptively still or moving very fast somewhere just beyond his range of vision. Oh yes, the Catcher was there all right, he could tell that now for sure. He was very close at hand. And yet the funny thing was, the surer he became the less it bothered him. In a way, he supposed, he had half expected it; much as if all his dodging and hiding were a kind of formal dance that they had somehow to do together, since they were the only ones who knew the steps; or as if they were heading for a tryst that both of them were bound to keep – reluctantly, perhaps, but with a curious sense of mutual under-standing. In a way, too, he preferred it when the enemy was declaredly on the move. It was action, and it was a challenge. Implicitly, he supposed, it was also a tribute to his work, and a proof of its importance: an aspect that of late he himself had been inclined – not to overlook exactly – but to place on the same footing as one or two others.

He hugged the package tightly to him, and made a careful mental survey of the situation, reminding himself in the curt, almost bossy manner he used for most of his messages to himself, that if he was to keep the testament safe, he must first and foremost keep his head. At all costs, he mustn't let his thoughts be hurried, or disturbed, or thrown off their course. That was point number one. Point number two was that he must avoid being left alone with the creature that was tracking him, or being jostled too close to him in a crowd, since either of these situations would favour theft on the Catcher's part. In isolated struggle, face to face and hand to hand, there was no question but that the Catcher would get the better of him and would drag the testament from his grasp by physical force alone. This might not have been true anything up to a week ago, he admitted, but it was definitely so now. He had no illusions as to his weakness. Indeed, there would hardly *be* a struggle to speak of now any more: the

Catcher would walk up to him, grab him, lay his hands on the manuscript and snatch it from him without further ado. If they were left alone, that is. In a crowd, where he could push, pull and jostle as much as he liked without arousing suspicion, he might also manage to take it by force (although perhaps with a little more difficulty, especially if Joseph put up any show of resistance), and would probably pretend that the package was his, not Joseph's, and try to win public opinion to his side by creating a nasty scene, and to corner him into a losing position that way. There was no telling what tricks he might get up to. No, crowds and solitude were both to be shunned. Point number three, therefore (consequence of point number two): he must keep calm, walk steadily on open ground, and keep his opponent from guessing his intention of boarding the vaporetto until the very last moment. If the ruse did not work on this first occasion, then he could, he supposed, go on embarking and disembarking all morning if necessary until he managed to dodge him. It would be a tiring business, of course, but not all that difficult, nor even dangerous. Or, if need be, he could go one further, and summon a private water-taxi, for he doubted that a child, however sinister and unchildlike his powers of command, would succeed in hiring a second taxi on the spot and in convincing its driver to take up a pursuit. So there were two relatively safe courses open to him by which he could reach San Lazzaro unmolested.

Which brought him to point number four. For once he had shaken off his enemy, there would, of course, be the final problem to face: that of finding a suitable resting-place for the testament in the library of the Armenian monks and of consigning it to a shelf unnoticed. There were lots of rare and valuable books stored there, he knew, but he suspected that for this very reason they would almost certainly be kept under lock and key, and that to put a volume in amongst them would be every bit as difficult as taking one out. This, however, was a problem that he would tackle when he came to it. First there was the dodging to be done.

Clasping the precious parcel under his arm more tightly than ever, he made his way towards the imbarcadero. A boat was just pulling up alongside, but it was going the wrong way; so instead of nearing the quayside, he paused in front of the picture gallery and made a show of consulting the notices that were pinned up outside. Having scanned the lot twice over and being unable to feign convincingly any further interest in them, he then crossed over to the bookstall by the ticket office and pretended to read the newspapers and magazines displayed there. It was, of course, vitally important that he should seem in no way to be on the alert, but he thought he could now risk a casual glance around him all the same, and pivoting slowly on his heels he let his gaze travel from the dark, wooden supports of the bridge (a little *too* dark to tell exactly what was going on beneath them), to the street behind; over the façade of the Accademia gallery itself, down the mouths of the two little corner alleys which branched off from the piazza on the far side, and across the canal and back to the bridge again.

As far as he could see, the general situation was promising: the Catcher had not yet ventured into the open, and another vaporetto, travelling in the direction he wished to take, was already in sight. Only a dozen passengers or so were gathered on the imbarcadero waiting to board, among them a girl with a push-chair. This, he noted pleasedly, more than promising was a real godsend. Wheeled vehicles of any kind were always taken aboard last of all, their embarkation being clumsier and requiring a certain leeway for manoeuvre; so if he stuck close to the push-chair and stepped on to the boat only just in front of it, there would not only be ample opportunity for him to keep track of any approach of the Catcher's from the rear, but time also for him to hop off again, exactly as he had planned, should he be followed on board.

Still careful to show no outward sign of hurry or even purpose, he moved slowly away from the bookstall and edged towards the ramp. The boat was drawing right in now, churning up the water as it ground into reverse and sending a great shudder through the raft on making contact; the mooring ropes were being fastened, the gears eased to neutral. He watched with bated breath as the last straggle of disembarking passengers stepped ashore, and saw the attendant hitch the safety chain to one side and signal to those waiting that it was now their turn. Now, he told himself bracingly, was the time to move.

Summoning all his strength for the final spurt, his eyes trained ahead to cover the foreground, ears and nose attentive to the rest, he accelerated abruptly and walked at a brisk marching pace – almost a run – along the gangway to join the tail end of the group; still half expecting, half dreading, to pick up the familiar scuffling sound of feet behind him or to catch another whiff of that characteristic tainting of the atmosphere that would announce the presence of his follower. But he heard nothing and sensed nothing, and preceding the push-chair with a smile of apology to the girl wheeling it as he brushed past her in his haste, he took a deep breath and stepped on to the deck.

When trying afterwards to reconstruct what then happened, he realized that he must at this point have been purposely tripped from behind (perhaps the Catcher had resorted to his long-distance hooking technique, for when his clothes were eventually returned to him he discovered that his trouser-leg bore a long, jagged tear at about ankle level), but all he now felt was a kind of disturbance behind him, as if he had got somehow entangled with the wheels of the push-chair, or a brake had been applied to one of his shoes. He tried to step forwards to keep his balance, but the leg bearing his weight refused to move, and by the time he had the presence of mind to lean backwards again and transfer it to the other, it was too late. He felt a rush of emptiness as he lunged forward, stiff as a ninepin with the effort of clutching the manuscript, and a kind of dull, painless implosion as he hit the deck. His last awareness – so dim as to be practically indistinguishable from the nightmares that followed – was a close-up of the grimy wooden surface of the deck, the white plastic wrapping of the manuscript some inches from his nose, and a small, greyish hand edging across the plastic and picking at it like a claw. Then, like a soft, velvet pall – covering everything, smothering everything, cancelling with a single, economic stroke his fears, hopes, worries, strivings and all the mental energy that had fired them – down came the dark.

XIV

THE VENICE in which Joseph found himself on regaining consciousness was different from the one, or the many, that he had known. It was a city within the city, an island within the island; and the isthmus which connected it to the respective mainland was a long, vaulted corridor to which he was not allowed access. The doctors and nurses were very firm about this. He had been caught, shortly after his admittance and in a still confused state, groping his way drunkenly down it towards the exit, and this rashly attempted escape had damaged his reputation among them and increased their vigilance. He had not been strapped to his bed, or anything drastically constrictive like that, but he had been led back their amid a great deal of fuss; the other inmates of the ward had been publicly primed to keep an eye on him; and now he could hardly put out a hand to readjust the blankets without one or other of them frowning at him and shaking their heads in disapproval.

Their disapproval, however, was lost upon him. After his first gesture of defiance he made no further attempt at flight, nor did he trouble the doctors with questions about his state, nor reply to any form of questioning from any source, but instead lay quietly on his back, his frame under the bedclothes scarcely troubling their flatness, and stared unblinkingly at the expanse of walls and ceiling above him.

The room was long and narrow, with two rows of beds on either side. It was painted the same watery green as his own, and the plaster in many places kept the same tenuous hold of the walls, but there all similarity ended. It was dry and stuffy and noisy, and lit by a relentless brightness that subjected every-thing it contained – beds, tables, charts, bottles, patients and staff alike – to a kind of mordant bleaching process akin to photographic over-exposure. From behind the wide, iron-framed, curtainless windows could be seen the tops of giant oleanders (these dry and blanched as well, for repairs were going on in one of the main wings of the hospital, and a film of builders' dust lay on all the surfaces in the vicinity – even, Joseph had noted listlessly as he drank from it, on the rim of the glass beside his bed) against a background of neatly aligned, newly tiled roof-tops, on which sat – likewise in tidy, symmetrical rows – not the pigeons or gulls that traditionally occupied such posi-tions throughout the rest of the city, but hosts of undersized and querulous starlings. In no aspect of the scene, in fact, neither in the buildings, the birds, the trees, nor even in the quality of the light itself, was there anything to remind him of Venice at all; and had it not been for the familiar pealing of the bells which forged at intervals a faint but recognizable link to the world outside, he might easily have thought that he had been trans-ferred while unconscious to another city altogether.

To a large extent, however, this feeling of strangeness stemmed from the fact that not only was it a different Venice that he found himself confronted with on recovering his senses, but in one important respect at least a different Joseph too: a vanquished, broken and utterly defeated one. Not that defeat in itself was that new to him, for he had known it well on all too many occasions, and over the years had managed to build up an opposite reserve of stamina and to discover various ways for the hoarding of it and for putting it into effect; yet during the first days of his stay in hospital, this hard-won quality of endurance did not come to his aid. In fact, he scarcely needed it. He just lay there silently in the hard, prickly bed, dressed in a strange, makeshift nightshirt which he had been provided with on entry, staring at the ceiling and existing despite himself; as inert and tensionless in mind and body as if he had been dilated in both beyond snapping point and then left to sag. He could see all right, and could hear the voices of others, but they seemed to come to him across a great distance, and the words, before they reached him, to melt into a meaningless babble of intermittent and wholly uninteresting sound. His own body was of no interest to him either. He could not help noticing that it was aching, but he noticed it resentfully, apprehending the ache as a ploy it was using to drag him back to an undesired state of awareness. If he ached, then he must be conscious, and if he were conscious, then he must think. And to think was what he did not want to do. The point had gone out of thinking.

This benumbed, semi-comatose state must have lasted several days, although he was unable to register or recapture any precise idea of its duration. While it lasted he was fed at various times, was led back and forth to the bathroom by an orderly, was given medicines, and was occasionally spoken to. For all he knew, he might even have answered, but he wasn't really aware of having done so, since, apart from his hazy perception of sounds and surroundings, and the gentle, almost objective sense of slipping away from them, all he was truly conscious of was the presence of a great, gaping hole somewhere within him as if an essential part of the machinery had been ripped out, and of the importance of not touching the hole, nor trying in any way to test how deep or wide it was: that, the wafting of the trees from behind the window-panes, and the play of light and darkness on the ceiling which signalled to him in an approximate fashion the passing of the hours and days. As regards the rest, he was nothing better than a puppet whose strings have been severed, or a doll that has been broken, stuck summarily together again with a piece or two missing, and then set aside. For this, of course, was not defeat as he had ever known it; it was rout and it was despair.

On the fourth or fifth day, however, these few bleak awarenesses were joined by another, and he began, imperceptibly at first but with a gentle, nibbling increase that brought him once more to the verge of emotional thawing-point, to miss Lapo and Emilio. During the visiting hour, he roused himself sufficiently from his torpor to scan the faces of the friends and relatives of the other patients as they peered self-consciously through the open doorway from behind bunches of flowers, wishing and half expecting to see his friend amongst them. The ward was full of other old men like himself, though – coughers and splutterers, and dressed in the regulation garb that spelt abandon – and there were few visitors who actually crossed the threshold. A young serviceman came for the noisiest cougher of all, and sat for a while on the bed in the far corner, looking silently down at his hands and coughing in tactful unison. A bossy, blustering couple arrived, pummelling at their relative's mattress and pillows, and dragging him up into a sitting position, brushing vigorously at his hair as if their own spruceness and comfort were at stake in the matter. Two children came with their mother and giggled and played hide-and-seek under the beds. But no Emilio.

Lastly, in the wake of the visitors, a young chaplain made a desultory round and paused at the end of each bed to ask if there was anything he could do to help; but this was not the visit Joseph had hoped for, and when his turn came he merely lifted an index finger and waved it at the man like a windscreen wiper until he left.

When the ward was quiet once more, he began to look around him with a little more interest. The bed to the left of his was empty, but he noticed that he had a neighbour to his right: a small, wizened gnome of a man with sharp, liquorice-black eyes and a woollen beret, who was now smiling at him connivingly, no doubt approving the short shrift granted to the chaplain. 'That's the way!' the man chuckled. 'Pussa via! Have no truck with the fellows. Feeling better today, then, are you?' Joseph smiled back and nodded. He *was* feeling better, he supposed; at least, he was feeling, and that in itself was something.

He lay back against the pillow and began cautiously to skirt his way around the damaged area inside, jabbing at its contours with the fastidiousness of a politician inspecting a bomb-site. What was it that had happened, to wound him so deeply? Not that he did not already know the answer. It was the testament, of course. It was missing. He had had it safely with him when he had stepped on to the boat; then had come the fall, and it had been with him no longer. That was what his feeling of void was due to: he had lost his testament. And with a sensation of bitterness so vivid that he could taste it like gall at the back of his mouth, the memory came slowly back to him of the dusty closeness of the deck, and of the white, shiny surface of the package with the dark, hooked fingers splayed across it. No, not lost it exactly: it had been stolen. That was what had happened. It had been torn from him mercilessly and taken by the enemy. So Pico had been right, then, after all, he thought sadly, venting a great, racking sigh that stirred the bedclothes for the first time that day; and he had been wrong. 'Qui operatur in Cabala, devorabitur ab Azazale.' Azazael existed. Azazael was greedy, and evil, and strong. And Azazael had won. He closed his eyes and tried by swallowing to get rid of the bitterness. If only, if only he had been more alert to the danger, he muttered to himself reproachfully; if only he had recognized it sooner. What a sorry figure he would cut if he were ever to be called to task on this account by a hypothetical tribunal of cabalist masters. What could he say in his defence? That he had not recognized the enemy in time because he had not believed in him? That he had had the misfortune to live in an age when devils were out of fashion? That this was why he hadn't been able to take the matter seriously? That he had been hampered throughout by his own ambivalent attitude – his own, stupid, wavering judgment ever leaning for comfort's sake towards a normality that had been of his own volition and his own making? What sort of a defence would that make? Normality, indeed! Why, there was nothing normal about the Catcher, nor ever had been. Nothing, nothing. Ever, ever.

He turned his head slowly from one side to the other, letting his face sink deep into the pillow in impotence and shame. Foolish, foolish, unforgivably foolish old man that he was. The knowledge and the power that centuries of cabalists before him had craved after, that they had striven for, and suffered for, and died for: these had been his. And after such effort to come by them, he had let them slip like worthless sand from his fingers and into the grasp of the enemy. He had betrayed his forerunners. That was what he had done. Betrayed them by his stupidity. In fact (and a shiver ran through him from scalp to heels as the realization dawned on him), perhaps he had done a worse and more terrible thing than to betray. For he remembered only too well now the chilling passage in the book of the Zohar concerning the 130th Psalm – the 'De Profundis' – where it was suggested that the well-known opening lines could mean not so much that Man had cried *up* to his God from his own lowly, earthly position, as (quite a different matter) that Man had cried *down* to Him. Not: 'Out of the depths have I cried unto You,' then. No. No. No. But: 'From out of the depths have I called You.' And this – worst of all sins of presumption and foolhardiness – was perhaps what he himself had done. Out of pride, out of ignorance, and with absurd and criminal blindness, he had perhaps gone and summoned a spirit of the underworld. If this was, in fact, the case, it was an error which deserved no forgiveness. Warnings against it had been plentiful and dramatic enough; they had run like a thread of burning wire through the works of every author he had ever consulted. And he, with his oh-so-superior wisdom, had disregarded them. Smiled at them. Put them down to childishness and superstition. Cabala summons angels, so his masters, all of them, had admonished, but woe to the incautious cabalist who invokes a star-demon in their place. And he, deaf to their warnings, blind to the dangers, and with a carelessness worthy of the greenest of novices, had abused the technique of Hokhmath ha-Tseruf, and brought about his own ruin.

He clenched both fists and drummed them angrily on the counterpane, making his knees bounce painfully, and welcoming the pain. Blundering old fool, he muttered angrily into the pillow; he should have taken what he had always looked on as the more colourful and trivial aspects of these doctrines more seriously. How he had used to scoff, for example, at the theory of the Demiurge. How he had pooh-poohed the idea of a misfired 'Tsimtsum'. How far-fetched it had seemed to him to think that the Creator could have overlooked some detail of security when He had recoiled into Himself to make place for His creation – as if the Godhead had been some kind of imperfectly sealed bag, or a negligent oyster! Such theories had used to strike him as nothing more meaningful than a series of badly mixed metaphors. And yet something not so *very* different from this must, he now realized, have actually happened. Either the Creator Himself had been imperfect, or else He must by mistake have left a loop-hole at some point, seeing that evil *had* got into the world. And not metaphorically, not negatively, not as a mere entry in the table of values; but concretely, bodily, as part and parcel of the stock. Oh yes, evil things existed sure enough, and not only had he come across one, but had in all probability been responsible for its awakening. Foolish, foolish, unnumbered times foolish magician that he was. He had realized far too late what the danger that threatened him consisted of; when he *had* recognized it, he had acted too late; and now he was too late, even, in repenting.

Or was he? At this point in his thoughts, a point which represented, so it seemed, the lowest ebb they would ever be capable of reaching, Joseph felt something quicken inside him — a vibration or jolt, as if the tiny parcel of his discarded hopes had touched rock bottom with just enough force to send it slowly surfacewards once more. With much puffing he pulled himself up into a sitting position and began to grope on the locker beside him for his glasses. Was it *really* too late, he asked himself again, a trifle more spiritedly? Must he really conclude that the enemy had got the better of him, merely because he had managed temporarily to come into possession of the manuscript? Had all the fight gone out of him of a sudden? Was he to give in like this without a struggle, crown his foolishness with frailty, and ruin the work of a lifetime, merely because the enemy had got the upper hand for the time being? No, surely not, he answered himself angrily. Surely not. But in order to fight back he needed to think things out carefully, and in order to think he needed his glasses. What had happened to them, he wondered? Had they broken when he fell? Had anyone salvaged them for him? And what about his wallet? And his toothbrush? He must have a toothbrush. He needed a pen and some paper, too; and his cigarettes (why, everyone in the vicinity, hospital staff included, seemed to be smoking all the time). He needed some small change as well, so that he could telephone Emilio and find out how Lapo was, and whether they could come and visit him and bring him what he needed. How long was he to remain here, anyway? There was nothing broken, surely, if he was not only allowed but even expected to go to the bathroom on his own two feet? And with a defiant twitch of the shoulders, he sat up straighter still and began rattling at the drawer of his locker – ineffectually, but with a shadow of his old vigour returned.

This sudden change of mood, although it seemed to please the doctors on their evening rounds, did not go down well with the rest of the ward at the time, and Joseph found himself once more under a keen scrutiny that he was now awake enough to notice and resent. At his every move a battery of eyes swivelled probingly in his direction (in fact, he discovered after a while that by holding his arms widespread and snapping the fingers of each hand in turn, he could actually manage to make them dance back and forth like those of the spectators at a tennis match); tongues clicked disapprovingly; noses sniffed; and his nightcapped neighbour, who had seemed until then the least wary of him and the most friendly, met his timid request for the loan of a few telephone counters with a curt refusal. The old man bristled with righteousness, his glinting little coals of eyes took on a suspicious glaze, the knitted bobble swung from side to side in denial, and, after much pleading on Joseph's part, in place of the counters he parted grudgingly with an eroded pencil and the back page of a newspaper, with which meagre booty Joseph had to be content.

For the rest of the day, the magician in him coming once more into the fore, he sat as upright as he could, his one, lumpy pillow wedged between the rim of his spine and the bars of the bedstead, his refound glasses – badly cracked in one lens – perched on the end of his nose, scribbling busily, on the margins of the paper, table after table of computation. A chore which kept him busy and, to the evident relief of the other occupants of the ward, kept him also relatively quiet. He was not bent on discovery, of course, but he was not just filling in time either. He was seeking confirmation. The method he used was one that he had borrowed from Agrippa and adapted from Hebrew to Ugaritic, adding a few little improvements of his own on the way, and consisted in constructing a double table – letters down one lead-column and across the base, numerical values of letters down another and across the top – in which the compiler (if, and only if, his values were correct to start with, that is, and he had remembered to calculate earthly things in hundreds, celestial in tens, and so forth) could then enter any name he pleased from either end – from the 'good' end, as maybe, or from the 'bad' one. If more information was needed, he could next re-enter it in the company of another name – either the Tetragrammaton itself, or the name of a somewhat lesser spirit, such as El or Shalim, or even the name of an archon (Katspiel or Domiel, for example, the guardians of the Sixth Palace).

He was familiar enough with the technique by now to have compiled the entire table with his eyes shut, but keeping them very wide open instead, and scratching the tip of the pencil in his old, invigorating way against his skull in order to titillate the brain inside, he set himself single-mindedly to his task; concentrating, however, despite a sneaking reluctance to do so, almost exclusively on the 'bad' side of the table.

When he had finished he eyed his results unhappily but with the tinge of grim satisfaction, stuck the pencil behind his ear, and crumpling the newspaper in disgust, threw it under the bed, ignoring the protests of the neighbour who had lent it to him. It was exactly as he had expected. The tables could yield nothing resembling a proof, of course – he didn't even know the child's surname, nor his date of birth – but proof didn't come into the matter. It was more a question of evidence. Little pieces of evidence dovetailing together. This was, as it were, the last feather in the tail, and it fitted smoothly into place: either directly or in the person of one of his henchmen (and it boiled down to much the same thing from the practical angle), it was Azazael he was up against.

Ha! Very well; Azazael be it then, he muttered to himself, polishing his glasses and reinserting them with a vigorous, almost flamboyant gesture on the bridge of his nose. So much the better. Let Azazael come. He had his name now, and his number. Let him come, and let him do his worst. There might be something faulty in the logic of this, but Azazael be damned. And might he be damned himself if he gave in so easily. Why, now that he had cleaned up his glasses, he could see that in the far corner of the ward someone had placed a Christmas tree. A Christmas tree meant Christmas, and Christmas meant the end of December. That was not late for his purposes. He might have months before him yet. He could remember Trevisan once telling him that hospitals did not like having dicey patients on their hands over Christmas: they made more work for the staff, he had pointed out baldly, and dampened the feeling of festivity all round. If this were so (and Trevisan seldom got his facts wrong on such matters), then he could perhaps count on a fairly prompt discharge, especially if he were to ask for it himself. Months were not aeons, but they were perfectly respectable periods of time. He could write the testament out again – that would not take too much doing, for he had it all by heart and most of it in note form as well – or he could track the Catcher down and try to retrieve the original manuscript. Besides . . . besides . . . Azazael, the child, the henchman, or whatever he was, would need time too. The work was long and complicated. It was full of riddles and pitfalls and side-tracks. No matter what preternatural powers of understanding his enemy might have, there was still the fact that in order to understand, he must comb his way through the material like any other reader. Not only this, but the last bulwark was still standing: there was still the safety device to rely on.

So the testament was not lost. It had merely come of age and was going its own way. He would have had to abandon it to its destiny shortly anyway, even if it had not been prematurely wrenched from him in this cruel fashion. Of course, he admitted with a shiver, the little grey claws were not the hands he would have chosen to leave it in (indeed it was hard to think of a less suitable pair), but sooner or later, more or less appropriately, into foreign hands it would have fallen. There was no call, surely, for him to despair? Azazael spelt only Azazael, after all, not necessarily defeat.

XV

NEXT MORNING, from the first seep of light onwards and although he knew perfectly well that Emilio wouldn't be there until mid-morning at the earliest, Joseph, his battling mood of the previous day still on him, watched the door for him. Every so often he would interrupt his watch to have a little chat with some of the other patients (for now that he seemed to have settled down a bit, they had softened towards him and had begun making small, shy openings of friendship, to which he had begun gratefully to respond), but then he would turn his gaze back to the doorway to take it up again, half fearful of having missed some sign of his friend's arrival in the interval. In view of the extraordinary piece of news which Emilio was to bring him, this eagerness was, in fact, to strike him later that morning as a trifle misplaced, but being a plain magician and no clairvoyant, he could hardly have known this at the time. He just wanted Emilio to come, and the sooner the better.

The nurse on night duty had told him that someone who answered very closely to his description (and, description apart, he reasoned, who was there to come, anyway, besides Emilio?) had been there twice already while he was still unconscious, and had sat by his bedside for more than an hour on each occasion. It was he, she explained, who had brought his glasses along for him, and he who had spoken to the doctors and had given them Joseph's name and address. As a matter of fact she and her colleagues had taken him for a close relative of his – a nephew, or more likely a son. Had they guessed rightly? And she had smiled at him expectantly, as if anxious for both their sakes that it should be so. No, Joseph had replied, sorry to disappoint her. No, not a son – not even a nephew; just a friend. But her words had cheered him up all the same: Emilio knew where he was and what had happened to him, had been in touch with the doctors on his behalf, and it could only be a matter of time before he returned. If not today, then tomorrow, or the day after at the outside, Emilio would be back. Of this he was sure. Yet, as he watched the row of languid old faces in the beds lining the opposite wall, all seemingly resigned to an endless wait for nothing and for nobody, he couldn't help worrying about ending up the same way himself, and found himself happier, all things considered, when keeping his eyes on the threshold.

When at long last he spotted Emilio's familiarly clad figure, which the acid brightness seemed unable to affect, save only to make it all the more solid and colourful in contrast to the rest, his heart changed rhythm and gave a sharp little castanet clack inside his chest: chiefly from the sheer joy of seeing him, of course, but in part, too, because of the suitcase he saw that he was carrying – a discordant detail which seemed to indicate that his friend had not come to fetch him, as he had perhaps rather foolishly been hoping all along deep down, but to bring his things and prepare him for a prolonged stay.

Emilio appeared to read his mind from a distance, and held up an open palm: 'Calma, calma,' he said softly, as he stepped into the ward and tiptoed with self-defeating lightness to the bedside. His face lit with the ill-repressed delight of one who brings good news and is about to tell it, he then bent down towards the pillow, his hand still open, and wiggled the central fingers under Joseph's nose. 'Uno, due, tre,' he explained excitedly. 'Three days. Only three days more and we'll have you back at the pensione with us again. I've had this direct from the matron, who has had it direct from the head of the department, and she tells me it's settled. Pensa, Joe – just think: you'll be home for Christmas.' And with a wide smile, he put down the suitcase with a thump and took the frail hand resting on the covers between his own, in a warm, friendly grasp.

Something about the greeting, or the faint trace of awkwardness which accompanied it, made Joseph suspect that the doctors had told Emilio more than the mere date of his dismissal, but he was so pleased to see him and to hear the news he had brought that he refused to let this bother him much. Returning the smile and the handclasp with all the strength he could summon, and shaking his head gently from side to side as though to precipitate its contents and allow them to settle, he closed his eyes, swallowed, and let out a sob of relief. For nothing else really mattered: Emilio was here; and he would be out by Christmas. Or, as Emilio had put it (and with him and Lapo waiting there to welcome him, the term no longer seemed quiet so inapt as it had until now), he would be home by Christmas. Now that they were numbered, the remaining days would pass in a trice. Three days. Seventy-two hours. The time it took a neophyte to meditate on the full name of the Creator, at the rate of a letter per hour. That was no time at all. He sighed again – deeply and contentedly.

Emilio watched all this in silence, evidently too moved to speak; then, running his hands through his hair and wiping them surreptitiously on his jersey, he turned away and looked benignly around him at the rows of curious faces, easing what would otherwise be an uncomfortable moment for both of them and waiting tactfully for the older man to recover his poise.

'Yes, three days more and you'll be out and about again,' he went on encouragingly after a short interval. 'Lapo has missed you, you know. He's getting on fine with me, but I know he'll secretly be glad to have you back. You're the one he likes best. I'd have brought him along here this morning, only I didn't think they'd let him in. Funny sort of rule, for a set-up like this, not when there are cats running free all over the place.' And he glanced around him in a friendly way, including the other patients in the beam of his attention. 'Rats, too, I shouldn't wonder,' he added by way of general incitement, his eyebrows comically raised. 'Topi, topi.'

This gambit was not well received: several heads turned towards him and eyed him severely, and one inmate – evidently out of loyalty to the place where he had spent so much of his time – went so far as to stiffen like a terrier and to spit at him a furious denial. But Emilio, taking it as a greeting, replied with a wave and a radiant 'Buongiorno' and turned back to Joseph well satisfied with the exchange. 'When you are feeling yourself again, Joe, we'll come back here together and cheer them up properly,' he whispered. 'A smile. A kind word. A little company. See? It does them a world of good, poveretti.'

Lifting the suitcase on to the foot of the bed, and whistling softly to himself during the silences, he chatted on, doing his best to make the one-sided conversation run with all the naturalness of a dialogue; and as he spoke, he rummaged through the case and began to produce its contents one by one with a little flourish of pride. 'Look, Joe,' he commented happily, 'tell me if anything is missing. Pyjamas. Toothbrush. Toothpaste. Sponge. Nailbrush. Soap. Slippers. Dressing-gown . . .' and he shook the black silk garment until it rippled, and draped it across the bed where it lay incongruously dark and dramatic against the pale, scrubbed cotton of the counterpane, with an 'Ehilà, this will impress your room-mates! . . . Now, what have we here? Ah, yes, reading matter,' and he gave a wink as he placed Joseph's casually acquired thriller on the locker. '*Vampiri e Vergini*. Just what you need. I didn't bring any of your other books because they seemed a bit heavy to me for convalescence, and a bit heavy for carrying too, but I can always bring a few round tomorrow if you like; when you're feeling stronger.' Here he stopped and looked at Joseph intently. 'How *are* you feeling, though, by the way? You don't look too bad to me, for someone of your age who has just taken a nasty fall. How did it happen exactly? And what were you up to, gallivanting around on your own at that time of the morning, eh?'

Joseph, who had been watching Emilio's every movement, basking more in the pleasure of his friend's company than in the actual recovery of his belongings, was taken a little aback by this question. Pleading loss of memory (which as regards the mechanics of the fall was perfectly true), he stammered a confused reply, and Emilio, again noting his difficulty and realizing that he must give his friend a little more time to rally, glossed over the awkward silence that followed by holding up another object and announcing in mock triumph: 'And just look what I have here for you: a get-well gift from our landlady – from the padrona di casa herself. I bet you never thought you'd receive such a mark of attention from the old witch, but there's nothing like illness for bringing out the best in my countrymen. She now goes around telling everyone you are her favourite boarder – *such* a gentleman; cosí Signore – and I shouldn't wonder if this were something she made especially for you, with her very own hands. She's been fiddling away with some funny-looking wool or stuff all week.' And he mimed the angular set of the padrona's head arched over her handiwork, crossing his forefingers like a pair of knitting-needles and making a fierce clicking noise with his tongue.

Joseph opened the package smilingly, infected by Emilio's glee. The smile, however, gave way to a gasp of open bewilderment when he found it to contain not a handmade garment of any description, but a small cotton vest or T-shirt with the drawing of an animal on the front. He looked closer, becoming more and more puzzled, and identified the animal as a dinosaur, painted moreover a bright shade of pink. Sinking back on the pillow, his shoulders beginning to quiver with laughter as he imagined himself trying to fit into such a ridiculous-looking thing, he spread it over his chest for Emilio's benefit and watched the dinosaur quiver in time to his laughter.

Emilio seemed just as nonplussed and just as amused. He pointed to it in stupefaction, buckled forward, clutching his stomach, and let out a splutter – so loud as to provoke the gnome in the next bed to hiss at him crossly to control himself: 'Un dinosauro! Un dinosauro rosa!' Then with an effort he straightened up again and tried, between minor splutters, to explain what had happened. 'No, no, no,' he corrected, his hands still pressed against his stomach and his face still struggling to be serious. 'Not her mistake: *my* mistake. This must be the present she gave me to take to the little boy. Wait a second while I find the right one for you – only I doubt it'll be an improvement,' and he rummaged in the case again to produce another similarly wrapped package of roughly the same dimensions.

Joseph took it from him without comment, but hesitated before opening it, and stretched out a hand for his dressing-gown instead. Aware of making a totally unwarranted jump to an unlikely conclusion, but pierced none the less by an icy dart of certainty, he drew the silk folds around him for warmth and protection and asked worriedly, all his amusement subsided: 'Little boy? *Which* little boy?'

'Oh, just some little boy who lives opposite the pensione,' Emilio explained easily. 'You're not the only one now who's causing a stir in the neighbourhood. There's this young Giuseppe, or whatever his name is, who has gone and caught some dreadful disease – meningitis, they seem to think.' He rubbed at his forehead and blew a commiserating gust of air. 'Poor little kid. There was an article on it in yesterday's paper, you know, and a whole lot of palaver as to whether the school ought to stay closed after the Christmas holidays. His mother used to work in the pensione once so the padrona feels personally involved in this case as well. It was before I moved in, of course, but maybe you remember her? And maybe you've caught sight of the child from your window? Nice little fellow, so they say. Well, never mind. I hope he'll be all right.' With this he began to rewrap the T-shirt, but noticing Joseph's pallor, laid it down again and leant towards him with an anxious frown: 'Are you feeling OK, Joe? Ti senti bene? Is anything the matter? Should I call the nurse or something?'

Joseph shook his head: it was nothing, he said faintly; just a moment's weakness; it would pass. And while Emilio, apparently reassured, went tactfully back to his task of unpacking and arranging his belongings, he sank down lower still in the bed, shut his eyes tightly, and tried to digest this piece of news. It had come as such a surprise and stunned him so completely, that he was hard put to know whether it was good news or bad, or really to take it in at all. So the Catcher had been taken ill. There was, he supposed, nothing so very extraordinary about that. Not in itself. But what lay behind it? Did it mean, for a start, that the child was right here in the hospital at this very moment? Presumably it did, from the way Emilio had spoken. In the second place, was he really suffering from meningitis or some similar, straightforward, physical disease? Or was it not more likely that the boy had meddled with the testament, and the safety device had sprung into action and was now having its effect? It could hardly be a coincidence, surely, the illness coming hot on the heels of the theft? What were the symptoms of meningitis, anyway? Headaches, he supposed; headaches and fever. Now, *could* the safety device be responsible for effects like that, he wondered? It was not what his studies had led him to expect, exactly, but then the statistics were few, and garbled, and unreliable almost to the point of worthlessness. There had been the Ausberg incident in 1512, for example, where the victim had been reported as having 'burst asunder', whatever that meant. No specific mention of this was made, but it would be fairly safe to assume that his temperature must have risen somewhat during the process. And then there had been the poor, inquisitive apprentice of Worms, whose punishment had almost certainly involved the head (amongst other things), although in a more spectacular way than by its aching.

So it could be the device, then, he supposed. But he hoped not. He sincerely hoped not. It was not what he had bargained for at all. He had known it was dangerous, of course, but when he had opted for it he had always imagined it somehow as working out its revenge at some remote time and place; never as acting within earshot, as it were, and on a victim whom for all his unpleasantness he had actually seen, and talked to, and to some extent known. Had this been irresponsible of him, he now wondered? Would he really have the courage to lie here passively and let things take their course, if what was involved was the suffering and death of a living creature – and a young one at that – of whose guilt, to be quite honest with himself, he was still not absolutely sure? For what if he had got it wrong about the Catcher, and the enemy he was dealing with was nothing but a cruel little child after all? When you thought it out carefully, the only proofs he had to the contrary were based on his own feelings. On suspicions. Intuitions. That day in the square when he had saved Lapo, for example: when he had looked the Catcher in the eyes and 'recognized' him. What had he recognized? What had he seen? A child at a window holding on to a piece of string with meat tied to the end. How had he 'known' at that moment that he was faced with some kind of supernatural being steeped in malice? What had his knowledge and recognition been based on? On his own feelings, of course. There you were again. Whichever way you looked at it, whichever way you turned, there were no proofs other than his own feelings to rest on: a vague sensation of stickiness when he had touched the child; an impression of having been stalked by him on three or four occasions; a thread of hair amongst his papers; and a nasty smell.

Yes, oh yes, he admitted worriedly, it was still possible that he could be wrong about the Catcher; and if he was, and the testament with its lethal contents had come into the hands of a mere child and was now pitting its spell against him, oughtn't he to step in immediately – no matter how unpleasant the child – and revoke the curse before it was too late? (Could he manage it, though? he wondered briefly. Could he even remember, without his books to consult, how it was supposed to be done?) Or was it not his prime and overriding duty to stick fast to his mission, and to save the testament at any price? That was what a proper magician would do, of course: save the testament. That's what a strong magician would do. An unprincipled one. Or, rather, one whose principles respected a nice, clear-cut hierarchy, and who never felt these terrible pricklings of doubt that he was feeling now. Ah, shilly-shallying old fool that he was, he wound up crossly: a magician who didn't know what he would do or what he should do, or even what he *could* do. That was what came of letting sentiment race ahead of reason: you came to an impasse and you stuck there. It was pointless to worry about duties and the like, until he had found out a little more of the facts. And with the brisk shake that he always used for getting rid of mental clutter of any kind, he heaved a sigh and slowly reopened his eyes.

Emilio had finished his unpacking. He had drawn up a chair, and was now sitting patiently beside the bed, watching him closely, the anxious frown of earlier still stamped on his forehead.

Joseph stretched out a hand and caught him urgently by the sleeve. 'Tell me, is the child here?' he asked. 'Here in the hospital, I mean?'

Emilio gave a slight start backwards. 'Mm-mm,' he nodded. 'He's here all right. But don't for goodness' sake go worrying about him. Try to get well yourself for a start. I'd never have told you if I'd thought it would upset you like this.' He smiled, and the frown lifted. 'I know what: I'll call in on him on my way out and take him the parcel as I promised . . . although I don't suppose he'll be needing it for a while yet . . . and then tomorrow I can tell you how he's getting on. How's that? Va bene così?' He shifted on his chair as if to rise, and then glanced down at his sleeve, which Joseph was still holding tightly, and gave a pointed little cough. Joseph clutched more firmly still. 'No,' he whispered hoarsely. 'Go now. I want to know now. Not tomorrow. Now!'

The request seemed to take Emilio by surprise, but he was evidently bent on humouring his sick friend (in fact, his readiness made Joseph wonder uneasily for a moment whether the doctors could have mentioned mental infirmity as well), and with an understanding nod and a brief squeeze of Joseph's arm, he went about his errand.

He was absent for a full five minutes, during which time Joseph, outwardly immobile but inwardly in a state of near-turmoil, clamped down a kind of temporary lid on the cauldron of his brain, and tried hard not to think at all. Nor did the cauldron's seething abate much on Emilio's return, when he reported that he had been unable to see the child, or the mother, or any of the doctors concerned. All he had been able to discover, he explained apologetically, noting Joseph's dismay – and this from an overworked and angry nurse who had taken him for a journalist – was that little Giuseppe was in the intensive care unit and was making routine progress 'as was expected'. A diagnosis of meningitis had not yet been issued, nor did it now seem likely that it would be, and there was no real call for alarm. That was all.

Joseph stared back at him vacantly, remembering only after a very long pause to thank him for his trouble and to ask him to sit down again, and scarcely noticing when, after a few minutes, Emilio rose and tiptoed out of the ward, urging him, as he went, to get some sleep, and promising to be back the next day. He was too busy with the cauldron. It had blown its lid properly now, despite his efforts to hold it down, and he could feel it bubbling over, scalding not only his mind, but his body as well.

He began to itch, and ache, and as the morning wore on, he shifted and tossed in his bed, and fretted, and with each change of position tackled the question of the Catcher afresh, as if hoping to discover this way a new angle on it or a better point of purchase. He questioned the doctors about him on their rounds; he questioned the nurses; he questioned the more mobile patients of his own ward, and even sent one of them as he had Emilio (although with much greater difficulty) to try to find out how the child was doing and what exactly was wrong with him. But to no avail. The only useful scrap of information that he managed to come by was the boy's surname; and using this, the borrowed pencil, and the jacket of his thriller, he set himself to construct an antidote, with which – ramshackle though it was – he felt he might at least be able to hamper the workings of the safety device a little, should it become necessary.

Although quite what he meant by 'necessary' he did not know, he admitted to himself wearily as he folded the scrap of paper and slipped it into his dressing-gown pocket; seeing that he still hadn't really decided between child and testament, which one took precedence from the moral point of view; nor even, from the practical angle, how far the saving of either was in his power to achieve. The crux of the matter, of course – far more simple than he wished to recognize, yet recognize it he must – was in the first place, that he could do nothing until he had seen the child for himself and had found out how ill he was, what illness he was suffering from, and whether the testament was responsible for it in any way; and second, that until he knew this he could not decide on the moral question either. Everything, therefore – actions, decisions, moral choices, the whole muddled caboodle – hinged on the one, clear certainty that he must see the Catcher; while the reverse side of everything – perplexities, hesitations, doubts and scruples – hinged on the same, clear but conflicting certainty that to see him was the very last thing he wanted to do.

XVI

WHEN THE lunch trolley, with his untouched meal on it, had been wheeled away, signalling by the dwindling squeak of its axles down the corridor the onset of the long, drowsy, central stretch of day during which even the most hardened old insomniacs would close their eyes and still their twitching and turn their coughs to snores, Joseph resolved to do something in person about quenching the cauldron.

Cautiously, so as not to ruffle the silence or disturb the sleepers, he edged back the bedclothes and swung his legs sideways, where they hovered stiffly above the slippers which Emilio had placed thoughtfully alongside until he bent them manually, and rose shakily to his feet.

'Hoh!' snorted the occupant of the nearby bed, roused either by the creaking of Joseph's knees or the faint gasp of pain that accompanied it. 'Jumpy today, aren't we? That's what comes of having visitors out of hours. No lunch; fidgeting all morning; I've been watching you. And where do you think you are off to now? Have they given you permission to wander around like that on your own?'

Joseph smiled apologetically but did not reply. He didn't feel much like conversation, and anyway he was saving what breath he had for the transit ahead, foreseeing it in terms of effort, if not of distance, to be long and hazardous. He had, as a matter of fact, asked permission to take a walk, and permission had been speedily granted. 'By all means,' the doctor had agreed, and Joseph had not missed the note of relief in his voice (confirming, he noted wryly, that Trevisan had been right about festivities and terminal illness). 'Faccia, faccia pure. Stretch your legs. Take a little exercise. Go anywhere you like, so long as you keep well covered and don't leave the building.'

So he reckoned he need feel no qualms on that account. He was stretching his legs, after all – very much so – he was wearing his dressing-gown, and he was (a little reluctantly) staying well inside the hospital. In fact, the only part of the doctor's advice which he could be accused in a certain sense of contravening was the injunction to go 'anywhere you like', since he was not going where he liked at all. Quite the reverse. He was going where he very strongly disliked, and what was more, he disliked the effort – both mental and physical – of getting there. Of the other numerous dislikes that lay beyond, he didn't even want to think.

Once he had got under way, though, he found that the effort wasn't at all unpleasant, but was good for him, and a stimulus. It was, in fact, quite exciting to find the creaky old machinery still in working order, and still able to meet the demands he made on it. He even found that with a little bit of self-hoodwinkery and by looking no further ahead than the tips of his slippers, he could manage to think of the interim goal of arrival as being the final one. And the further he progressed towards it the easier his progress became, and the more confident he began to feel.

When he reached his actual destination, though – a heavily padded swing-door, bearing the somewhat sinister lable 'Ri-animazione' – and had found, inside the unit itself, the room he had been looking for, his confidence wavered, and left him abruptly; and he lowered himself down on a bench facing the doorway and stared at it hard, trying to pluck up courage enough to enter.

The door was ajar, and the room beyond in darkness. He looked quickly down at his slippers again: the darkness needed thinking about, he realized, for it was not exactly what he had expected. He had braced himself for the Catcher – hopefully a weaker and more subdued Catcher by now – and for a face-to-face meeting with him, but not for a get-together in the dark.

No, not for anything quite as problematical as that. He gave a little shiver, and went on looking at his toes.

As he sat there, undecided as to whether to spare himself the actual business of entry and try to obtain information in a less direct way from a passing nurse or doctor, or whether to brave the darkness (which might be preferable to light, anyway, he reasoned: less informative, but preferable) and take a quick look into the room, the door swung open and a young nurse came out on tiptoe, a Thermos in her hand. When she saw Joseph she raised her eyebrows enquiringly, and on hearing his mumbled request as to the child's progress and noting the intense anxiety with which it was made, gave him a wide smile in answer. Placing him evidently as a relative or close friend of the family, she took him by the sleeve and led him gently into the room. 'Vada, vada,' she whispered encouragingly, giving him a slight push and half closing the door behind him. 'Go and see for yourself.'

Once inside, Joseph stood absolutely still and blinked several times, until, by the slice of light coming from the corridor outside, he was able to make out where the bed was. Finding himself uncomfortably close to it, he side-stepped, and without thinking further went straight to the window, which was visible in faint outline on the far side of the room, and groped in the penumbra for a handle or knob of some kind. Having found one, he opened the window wide enough to allow a finger of light to enter, and went back to the bedside. All his nervousness had left him. He felt calm all of a sudden, and resolute, as if in the short space of time that had passed since he had left his sick-bed and by the mere fact of being upright and mobile again, all his magician's power and savoir-faire had been restored to him. In fact, he could hardly remember what all the dithering had been about or how it could have arisen. It was, after all, such a simple matter: he would be able to tell at a glance – or, at the very worst, a touch – whether the disease was magical in origin or not. All that was needed was a quick, neat assessment of the way things stood – a peep under the covers, a hand on the brow, or over the heart – and then (or not, as may be) a rapid revocation of the curse. It was as simple as that. To make matters even easier, too, he could sense none of his former repugnance to draw near the child: the room smelt fresh and clean, his own heartbeat was steady, his breathing easy, and the inflowing shaft of light revealed merely a small, still, innocuous-looking form under a pale blue coverlet, from which no waves or sensation-producing currents whatever seemed to emanate. Fingering the scrap of paper in his pocket on which he had scribbled the closest thing to a recision procedure that he had been able to produce without the help of his books, he drew closer to the bed.

In doing so, however, he received two shocks in quick succession — the second of particular violence. The first shock was when from the far side of the room, still curtained by shadow, a voice spoke up softly and said: 'Grazie, Professore. The nurse said to open the window just a little now that the crisis is past, and that will do fine. Just look how he's sleeping, povero bimbo.' And looking guiltily across the room, he saw the Catcher's mother sitting quietly in a chair in the corner, watching over her son's sleep, and looking badly in need of rest herself. 'How nice of you to come and see us — when I know you have been so poorly yourself.' She added politely: 'I was told you'd been asking after him, and I can't tell you how I appreciated it. Everyone's been so kind, really.'

To this, Joseph was too abashed to make a reply, but the young woman seemed so pleased to see him and so unsurprised at his opening the window like that, unasked, that this particular shock did not last long. What did, on the other hand — and not only last, but confound him so utterly at the time that he had to lean and steady himself on the rungs of the bedstead to stop his head spinning — was that the boy sleeping so peacefully under the covers was not only untouched by magical influence of any kind (a fact which ought to have relieved him, had he been able to take it in), but he was not the Catcher.

The light revealed this beyond any possibility of doubt: the hair, in the first place, was not dark, but a clear, reddish-gold colour; the face that lay against the pillow was visible in profile only, but it was unmistakably light-skinned, snub-nosed and freckled. A chubby, rather ordinary face. Vitamin-fed. Innocent-looking. Joseph remembered seeing it – or something very like it – before, and when he looked closer he knew where. Yes, he had seen it in the photograph of her husband so proudly displayed in the woman's apartment. This was their son all right. The carabiniere's son. This was Giuseppe. The boy whose bedroom faced his own. But it was not the Catcher.

This bald but inescapable fact landed in his brain with the effect of an eagle in a dovecot, scattering the other facts stored there into a state of flurry and flight which Joseph could see at present only one way of reordering. 'Your other son, though?' he asked quietly, doing his best to make the question sound as normal as it ought to at face value. 'How is he?'

'The baby? He's all right, thank goodness,' the mother replied promptly. 'He's with my husband's family in Mestre, and we'll soon be joining him there. It wasn't anything catching after all, the doctors say – just some kind of fit or convulsion – so the moment Giuseppe can leave the hospital I'm taking him back to Mestre.' She gave a shamefaced laugh and tossed her head in the pony-fashion Joseph remembered from their previous meeting: although the fringe, greasy now from inattention, no longer swung but stuck to the forehead and went with it. 'You've heard about the flat . . . I told you, didn't I? . . . how it's supposed to bring bad luck? Well, I don't really believe it, of course – not even after this – but I'll tell you one thing: however stupid of me it may seem, I'm not going back there.' And she made a lightning sign of the cross, kissed her thumb, and then hid it behind her, looking even more shamefaced than before. 'Never again,' she whispered, this time more to herself than to Joseph. 'Never again. And that's that.'

Although this confession of hers intrigued Joseph for a moment, and although it started up that spidery little tickle at the base of his skull which he had felt before on similar occasions when something of importance claimed for an attention he was unable to grant, it was not at all a satisfactory answer to his question. Giving an automatic scratch at the nape of his neck, so eager for the reply as to let slip his mask of unconcern and make no attempt at righting it, he went on slowly: 'No, I wasn't thinking of the baby. I meant your other grown son. The one who sleeps in the room opposite mine. The dark one. The one I see setting off to school in the morning with the other children following, who I always think of as the . . .' Here he checked himself, trying to think of a kinder term than the one he had been about to use, and trying also to steady his voice. 'As the ringleader of the group.'

The young woman's face wrinkled into a frown and, biting on her lip, she was silent for a moment and looked hard at Joseph, as if to gauge his earnestness. 'But I haven't got another son,' she said at length, 'and there aren't any other children in the building. It must have been Giuseppe you are thinking of. That's his room, and he's the one that goes to school in the mornings.'

'No, I am not thinking of Giuseppe,' said Joseph more firmly. 'I have often seen a boy – quite a different boy – in that very room. Perhaps Giuseppe has a friend who visits you there, and it is this friend of his I have seen. Please think carefully. The matter is of great importance to me. A dark-skinned, dark-haired boy of about the same age with narrow, rather slanting eyes?'

The mother shook her head again, looking at Joseph with a subtly altered expression: puzzled still, but to a different degree and evidently for a different reason. 'I think you must be mistaken,' she replied gently. 'There's never anyone there but the three of us. Giuseppe doesn't bring his friends home with him as a rule, and since he lost his father he doesn't spend much time there himself. Most days he's out playing football. Don Gianni has rigged up a kind of pitch for them behind the church – I expect you've seen it. It's not a real pitch, of course; not half big enough, but it's somewhere for them to play and get a bit of fresh air. No, I think you are making a mistake.'

As she said this she rose to her feet and drew closer to Joseph, looking at him very worriedly indeed. 'But you shouldn't be tiring yourself like this, Professore. You should be back in bed. Let me call a nurse and have her accompany you back to the ward. It was good of you to come and see us, it really was, but perhaps it was a bit too soon for you to walk all this distance on your own.' She placed a hand under his elbow and, sensing his unsteadiness, led him over to the chair she had been sitting in and lowered him gently down into it. 'Just stay here for a moment and rest, while I go and fetch someone.'

Joseph was by now too bewildered and too reckless to care whether his behaviour be put down to illness, or to weak-headedness, or even to both. Instead of sinking obediently into the chair, he clung fast to her arm and made a last, desperate bid for clarity. 'Does your son . . . ?' he began, in a strange, growly tone which he could hardly recognize as his own. 'Please do not think . . .' he went on, nearly an octave higher, 'I know the question may sound odd . . . but does your son wear a brace in his mouth? A dental brace? One of those metal contraptions for straightening the teeth?'

He realized immediately that this was a mistake. The young woman sighed and pulled away from him, and pressing a bell on the bedside table, backed steadily towards the doorway. Her voice when she spoke was no longer gentle. 'I think you are tired, Professore. And, please excuse me, but I am tired too. This is the first real rest Giuseppe has had in days and I want to take advantage of it and get a little sleep myself. Come back and see him tomorrow, if you like, when you are feeling a little stronger. He'll be sitting up then, and you can have a talk to him, and ask him about this friend of his you think you have seen. His memory is better than mine, so perhaps he'll be able to help you more than I can. And now, if you don't mind, I think you really ought to be getting back.'

Joseph nodded silently. A purposeful-looking nurse had now entered, in answer to the summons, and after a whispered but blunt consultation between the two women, which took place across the top of his head, he let himself be led by her igno-miniously back to his bed.

He was so shaken by what had happened that he hardly recognized it when he reached it, and sat for some time on its edge, staring vaguely about him, before realizing that he was expected to get back in. His neighbour let out a gleeful chuckle at seeing him return from his outing in such a disorientated state, but he didn't pay much attention to this either. The riddle of the Catcher lorded it over all else. In the first place, if he was not the child who lived across the way, then who was he? Or, more fundamentally still, if a shade elliptically: was he? Did he exist, that is? Was he real? Or was Azazael, the dark child, a product of his own imagination alone? (This last was, of course, a rooted and – as far as possibilities could be so described – an increasingly concrete possibility; although why his imagination should have fitted him out with the bizarre attributes of a dental brace and a nasty smell was a question that seemed in need of a second and quite independent kind of answer.) Just how many of his memories concerning the creature could he rely on as having really taken place? In the world of objects? The outside one? And how many could he demote from material status if he were honest with himself, and allow as having possibly taken place in his own imagination alone? Still more worrying, and harder to answer: how far and how clearly were the two theatres of happening – world and head – separable from one another at this stage? (By which high-flown concept, he supposed wryly, what he meant was: was he going mad, or had he already gone so?) And these were only half the questions. For seen from the other angle – granted, that is, that the theatres *were* separable, that his memory *was* reliable, and his hunches right and his reasoning solid (in short, if he was not mad at all but perfectly sane) – then not only who was the Catcher, and what was he, but *where* was he? What was he up to now? And, last but not least: what had he done with the testament?

XVII

S O THE sick boy, the boy who lived in the room facing his own – and unless the mother was mistaken about this or deliberately misleading him, the one and only boy who lived there – was not the Catcher after all. It is hard to explain exactly what this discovery brought about in Joseph's already befuddled mind, especially now that we have shifted (somewhat capriciously it may seem, although there are reasons for it, and we shall be nosing our way inside again very shortly anyway) to the more distant and perhaps most unrevealing position of all: that of outsiders looking neither in nor around, but looking back. Earlier we compared its impact to that of the landing of an eagle in a dovecot, but the kind of lightweight confusion which this brings to mind smacks of understatement. It did not flurry him: it floored him. It knocked him sideways. To rotate the metaphor still further, it turned his world upside-down, and with a violence that is hard to grasp seeing that he normally had little difficulty in digesting facts – most of them just as curious and many just as sinewy. In fact, over the years he had stomached a whole host of them with the ease of a boa-constrictor. He believed in magic, for a start; he believed in the supernatural; he believed in goodness, and with a touch of reluctance had come tardily round to believing in evil. A little more reluctantly, but without actually digging his feet in and balking, he believed in devils too, towards the end. What more natural, then, than that he should go one step further in the same direction and credit his devils with powers to confuse appearances, to mislead their enemies, and to convince them that they have seen things and touched things and known things that they have never seen, nor felt, nor known at all? And yet this was just what he was not able to do. It was not the way his mind worked, and not therefore the way it thought that other minds should – or could – work. Not his own or other bodies, either. Azazael could possess a body, he granted, or could possess someone else's body, but he couldn't whisk one into being and then whisk it away into nothingness again. Not even the Creator Himself could do a thing like that. The question of madness faded to one of purely academic interest in comparison. It was not even that pertinent any more. After all, he had seen the Catcher with his own eyes, hadn't he, day after day, and night after night? Eyes might play tricks, of course . . . there were the well-known 'arguments from illusion', and so forth . . . but he had not only seen him; he had smelt him, and grappled with him, and had been robbed of his testament by him. These were very concrete happenings, calling – so he felt – for equally concrete explanations, and he was in no way prepared to end his life-span – however short the amount of it that remained – with the explanations missing and the riddle unsolved.

Unfortunately, as far as his investigations were concerned, the span that in fact remained to Joseph at this point was very short indeed: most of it to be spent in that passive, tedious condition of bedridden convalescence, so unsuited to the leading character of any narrative, to which he had by then become accustomed, if not resigned. And it was from this handicapped position that he had to carry out his detective work for the next few days, his only feeler to the outside world – apart from mere speculation – being the ever-helpful and ever-loyal Emilio, who would bring him his meals, report pieces of local gossip, and, when he had time to spare and Joseph courage to ask, even run the odd errand for him as well – odd indeed though such errands must have seemed to him in some cases.

Not only must we stick by Joseph, however, and brave the tedium of yet another chapter or so featuring an inert and horizontal hero, but we must, as warned, move in closer in order to observe from the correct angle one fairly interesting fact that he discovered while thus bedridden, and a number of very interesting ones that came to his notice during the short and ultimate period of mobility that followed.

On Christmas Eve he was allowed to leave the hospital. He was weak still and covered the distance to the nearest ferry with a certain amount of effort, leaning heavily on Emilio's arm, and looking round perplexedly at the city that re-embraced him, surrounding him once more with its familiar landmarks, as if it were destined to remain for ever alien to him now, and for ever remote. The great equestrian statue of Colleoni, for example, that confronted him as soon as he stepped outside the portals of the hospital; this must have been so well known to him by now as to merit scarcely a glance. Yet not only did he glance at it but stood looking at it earnestly for minutes on end, frowning into the belligerent eyes of the bronze condottiero as if aware of them for the first time, tilting his head to one side, chewing his lip in concentration, and staring and staring until Emilio coaxed him gently away. An imaginative onlooker might well have thought that he had read there a warning, or a message of personal hostility towards himself, so shaken did he look as he resumed his walk. Although a perceptive one would have seen that, more than downcast or perplexed, he was simply dazed: the way a sleepwalker is when roused too abruptly, or a man when he has been blindfolded, spun in circles, and then suddenly exposed to sunlight again.

For the main part of the return journey, the dazedness stayed with him. He hung on to Emilio like a child; watched uncomprehendingly but with interest while he bought them their tickets; and as the boat that carried them homewards threaded its way through the basins of the Arsenale, he kept turning his head bewilderedly from bank to bank, apparently struck not only by the scenery but by the mere fact of finding himself afloat.

When they disembarked and made slowly towards their own neighbourhood, however, some inkling of familiarity and some vague sense of belonging began at last to return. It could hardly have been otherwise, for the minute square with its shops and trees and shiny, worn paving-stones seemed to bask in a glow of unmistakable welcome, and the narrow alleyways to have spread themselves with kindly forethought to accommodate their passage. Three cats dozed peacefully in the warmth of a filtering sunbeam, and an old woman sat outside a doorway with a bowl in her lap throwing little scraps of food in their direction. She smiled at Joseph as he passed: 'Ben tornato, Professore.' Welcome back.

Emilio, worried by his friend's strange, faraway mood and anxious to shake him out of it as soon as possible, saw his chance and expanded on this. 'There you are, Joe. I told you that Italians are at their best when anyone's ill or anything. It's a common enough saying, but it's perfectly true. All the neighbours have been asking after you: the old girl in the bar, the waiters in the restaurant, the shopkeepers, the lot. Your illness has made you popular.' He nudged Joseph's elbow to stir him and transmit his own enthusiasm. 'People are *glad* to see you back. Of course,' he added in afterthought, looking away, 'it doesn't go on working if you are ill too long, or too often.'

'Ah,' said Joseph steadily, giving thought to the matter, 'well, I doubt I shall lose their sympathy that way.'

Emilio stole a sideways glance to see how this was intended. 'Ssssh, Joe,' he chided with a hiss, squeezing his arm and staring hard into the window of the shop they were passing, 'of course you won't. And I'll tell you why. Because you are going to get well – and quickly, that's why.' And steering the conversation towards the brighter topic of how pleased Lapo would be to see him back, he led him carefully down the last stretch of alleyway and up the slippery steps of the pensione itself.

In spite of these predictions, however, Lapo did not seem to be delighted in the least. He was lying at the top of the staircase when they entered, and not only did he stay there, but seemed, as Joseph drew closer and held out a hand to caress him, to shrink back and to bare his teeth in the awakening of a snarl. (Although it was just possible, thought Joseph in hurt surprise, that the snarl, if not the shrinking, might have been due to a trick of the light.) He sniffed suspiciously at the outstretched hand, and to make it quite clear whose side he was on now, turned his head aside and glanced appealingly at Emilio as if asking his advice on whether to repulse this forward old stranger or to put up with him. The moment was an awkward one. Emilio's tact, deployed with such success on other, trickier occasions, seemed to desert him. 'Lapo, *Lapo*!' he scolded, making no attempt to minimize what had happened or to try to explain it away. 'What's got into you, for God's sake? It's your master: Joseph. He's back. Guarda!' And taking hold of the dog's muzzle he twisted it forcibly towards Joseph's torn trouser-leg and held it there; determined on getting some show of recognition out of him, but obtaining nothing more friendly than a faint rising of the hackles along the animal's backbone. Of the three, it was Joseph who appeared to mind the least about this curious little incident (although inwardly he was probably the worst offended and the most deeply stirred by it), and he who put an end to it with a shrug of his shoulders, putting a restraining hand on Emilio's and urging him to let matters be. Then, stepping calmly over Lapo without looking at him, he made for his room.

With a last cross look at the puppy, Emilio followed him inside, and helped (to Joseph's patent dismay) by the landlady and the Signora, who had been standing waiting like sentinels on either side of the bed, began to unpack for him. Elbowing him aside, however, the two women took charge of the practical details. When they had finished with the case they took hold of Joseph himself, and with a duet of awed murmurs, sucking in their breath, and exchanging shocked comments now and again on his thinness and altered appearance – 'Poveretto, come che el xè ridoto! Look at those legs! What have they been feeding him?' – as if his stay in hospital had made him not only weak, but deaf as well, they partially undressed him, ignoring his protests with good-natured but total unconcern, eased him into a pair of freshly laundered pyjamas, damp and soapy as a flannel, and tucked him, with gusto, tightly into the bed.

Joseph glanced from the bed to the smiling faces that now

hovered above it, proud of their achievement, and then back to the bed again. The reception had been so smooth and so rapid that his one true wish – that of being allowed to remain dressed and seated – could no longer be expressed. He noticed that he had been given an extra blanket, and murmured his thanks. He would need it, he realized. The room was colder than he remembered it as being – perhaps the oven-like atmosphere of the hospital had disarmed him in this respect – and there was a dank, closed feel about the place, aggravated by a mouldy, faintly greasy smell that had never been there before. He turned an incurious gaze towards the shelves on which his books were stored (his own books, he reminded himself; the irreplaceable, beloved companions of a lifetime; the only possessions he had ever really cared for – and with what passion and intensity he had once cared) and saw, without a twinge of displeasure, how dusty and neglected they had become. Once their mere presence would have been enough to give him a sense of security and warmth, but now all they gave him was the impression of not lying in a bedroom at all, but in the corner of some unvisited library or forgotten archive.

With scarcely more curiosity, he then shifted his gaze to Emilio who, having ushered the ladies to the door, had dragged Lapo down the corridor and over the threshold and was now making a brave attempt to persuade him to remain inside. It was only too clear to all three of them that the attempt would not succeed. As on the eve of Joseph's departure, the puppy hung close to the door with his nose pressed against the frame, and each time Emilio opened it to make an exit, Lapo plunged forward into the breach, wriggled a passage through it with much bunching of the skin, and slipped relievedly into the corridor outside. At the fourth escape, Emilio gave up trying. 'I don't know what's got into him, Joe,' he said miserably. 'The silly creature. What can it be? He doesn't even seem to recognize you any more.'

Joseph shrugged, and gave his upside-down smile. Personally, he had an idea that the animal's behaviour towards him was not due to failure of recognition at all, but to some other, quite different and possibly deeper cause. What it was, though, he could not imagine, nor did he much wish to try.

Once left alone, he wormed his way out of the jacket of his pyjamas (the trousers were too severe a challenge), threw it more from habit than from conviction in the direction of the radiator, and abandoned himself to the mattress and his thoughts: macerating in both and drawing from them much the same relief that he would have got from an acid bath. The Catcher. Azazael. Oh, he thought miserably, the worry of it all. The testament. His entire life's work. What had become of it now? What would become of it in the future? Did it even *have* a future? And if not, how much time was there left in which to remedy matters and produce a duplicate? And how much strength? He gazed listlessly at his hands as they lay splayed before him, palms downwards, on the blanket, and flexed the fingers one by one. Magician's hands. Powerful hands – or had been once. Would they perform this last service for him still? If the worst came to the very worst, would they copy out the testament for him all over again? Would they last that long, though? And would their owner?

As if in reply – and not a very consoling one at that – he was visited by a fit of coughing worse than any he had ever experienced: the springs of the bed recoiled under its impact; the air rang with his raspings and barkings; and on the far side of the room (uncanny but perhaps unconnected phenomenon) the curtain swung – gently at first – and then billowed forwards into the room with the fullness of a spinnaker on a ship under sail. And while he lay there trembling, trying to get his breath back, the shadow of the palazzo, with the darker patch of the Catcher's window at its centre, danced before him through the veil of curtain; goading him, taunting him, and setting his thoughts on a related but slightly different track.

The palazzo. Hmm. What was it that the Catcher's mother had said about it? . . . No, poor woman, he corrected himself hastily: not the Catcher's, the other boy's mother . . . What was it she had said? 'Porta rogna', that was it: it brings bad luck.

Well, it certainly had to her, he thought sadly; her husband killed, and her child in hospital. Poor woman, indeed. But it must have taken more than that, surely, to give the place its bad name; and it must have taken longer, too, than the few months that had passed since her husband's death. So perhaps she had had a point there, with her half-confessed superstitions and her sketchy little sign of the cross. He hadn't given the matter much thought at the time, but perhaps the evil really was lodged, not so much in the people that lived there, as in the house itself. Perhaps the palazzo was nothing less than some kind of diabolical headquarters: Azazael's Venetian residence, so to speak, and the centre of his operations. It was a far-fetched hypothesis, he had to admit, but it was a very worrying one. Very worrying indeed. The nearness of the house to his own lodgings, for a start: that could hardly be a mere coincidence. And if you ruled out coincidence, then it must either mean that Azazael had been spying on him and scheming against him for much longer than he thought, or else that his own choice of dwelling had been influenced, if not actually determined, by the fact of the nearness (depending, of course, on who had moved in first). Neither alternative was very comforting, but that was no good reason for discarding the hypothesis.

And yet, he thought a little sadly, he could still remember how beautiful it had once seemed – this looming, graceful building with its peeling plaster and its blackened window. In fact, that, if anything, had been why he had chosen this spot when he had been looking for rooms: because he had liked the look of the place. It had never seemed *evil*, surely, until now? Decaying, yes; home of the Catcher, yes; upsetting in the end on both these accounts, but never evil. Could he then actually have been tricked into thinking it beautiful, to make him come and live here? Or had he failed to see what it was really like simply because – short-sighted old fool that he'd always been – he had never understood the first thing about evil and had never been able to recognize it in any of its forms?

He peered searchingly at the dark, rectangular shape of the window, clearer now that the curtain had swung itself to a standstill; and the harder he looked the more plausible it all seemed. It *was* an evil-looking place. He could see that now. It was definitely creepy. There were those odd little windows, too, dotted around, quite out of line with the regular floors – some he had never seen opened at all, some boarded up, and some bricked in completely. And one of them was only a few feet to the left of the Catcher's window. Of course. How stupid of him. There could easily be a secret room behind it, he now realized: a hiding-place in which the stolen manuscript might be stowed away, or where the Catcher himself might still be camping out.

So what he must do now, was to go back there and make a proper search. That's what he must do. Although not – thank you very much – until he was feeling strong enough to face whatever it was that he might find there.

XVIII

CHRISTMAS over, for three days running Joseph kept to his room. Unwillingly, now that he knew where he ought to be instead, but he kept to it; lying solemn-faced in his bed, resting himself up with a single-mindedness that at times almost threatened to tire him, so hard did he go about it. With his alarm clock at his elbow, his glasses off, and his head thrown well back so as to avoid any reminder reaching him of the house behind the curtain, he would spend the first fifty minutes of each hour in enforced relaxation. When the alarm rang, as if himself set to clockwork, he would flex his muscles under the blankets, bend his joints one by one, do his breathing exercises, and take a short walk round the room. Then, as the minute hand came round to twelve, he would check the rate of his breathing, count his heartbeats, reset the alarm and start all over again.

Long- or even medium-term plans no longer interested him, his former goal of lasting long enough to retrieve the manuscript, or to rewrite it if necessary, having been ousted by the simple, compulsive desire to get back inside the palazzo and see what was going on there. What worried him now was the immediate problem of stairs, and how to climb them with such shaky legs and unpredictable knees. There was the brain to be rested too, of course – a task which, thanks to the window opposite, ready to spring on him every time he replaced his glasses, he found every bit as difficult and every bit as tiring. In fact, had it not been for the odd diversion now and again that helped him take his mind off things, it would have been an impossible one. But, as Emilio had predicted, people seemed genuinely pleased to see him back, and, to his surprise, he received a number of visits. Faces – some of which he was at a loss to place – would peer round the doorway, a trifle inquisitively, but wearing the kindest of smiles. The day before, for example, a whole procession of elderly men like himself had trooped in from the bar, bringing him a bottle of his favourite wine. Early that morning two women clad in black had knelt at the foot of his bed, and recited the rosary with tears in their eyes. (A little tactless of them, he had thought at the time, but again, extremely kind.) The Signora, on a worldlier note, had lent him her portable radio. And in the evenings Emilio had taken to bringing along his basset horn, and would plump himself down on the foot of the bed and practise there at length, making a noise which Joseph found rather soothing, while he turned the pages for him.

Lapo, too, brought him comfort of a kind – all the more welcome, because unexpected. Still on no apparent grounds, he seemed to have forgiven Joseph his absence or whatever it was that had caused the mistrust between them, and on the evening of Joseph's re-entry had returned to his place by his master's bed. It had happened like this: the door had swung open a few inches, and Joseph, with tears in his eyes, had watched the seal-like blob of the dog's nose and the thick, vibrating whiskers worm their way round the panel. After sitting there apologetically on the threshold for a minute or so, nosing the air and blinking, Lapo had appeared to come to a decision. Squirming snake-wise, slowly at first and then faster and more confidently, he had made his way to the bedside, and with a high bound, as if clearing some invisible obstacle in his path, had leapt on to Joseph's stomach and had splayed himself over it like a bearskin. Joseph had grasped out blindly and drawn him into his arms, whispering the ciphered name over and over again, unable to check the tears which were by now running down his cheeks and dripping with a series of faint thuds on to the fur below; very thankful at the same time that no one was watching. It was such a small thing to be moved by, a dog's approval. And he supposed that was why it moved him: by its smallness.

Since when, the dog had only left his side for brief walks and for food and drink, and spent the rest of the time steadfastly glued to the bedside, watching, mainly sleeping, accompanying him on his therapeutic trips round the room, and then settling down again on the floor alongside, within touching distance of his hand – an arrangement that seemed to suit them both very well.

By the third day of his resting scheme, Joseph was feeling strong enough to carry out a little further investigation, and leaving aside the alarm clock and his exercises, he set himself instead to the distasteful task of drawing a picture of the Catcher, with the idea of giving it to Emilio and sending him to make a few routine enquiries – to the bar, and to the imbarcadero where he had fallen. He thought it was unlikely, but there was still a chance that someone besides himself had seen the elusive, dark child as he had gone about his business, and it seemed a shame not to check on this. The actual drawing of it cost him untold effort. Drawing had never been a strong point of his, not even at the best of times, but now, with the times and the subject in his disfavour, the closer he came towards achieving a likeness, the more his pencil seemed to disobey him and thwart his intentions, and the clearer the image of the face came before him in his memory, the less inclined he felt to draw it. In the end, however, with patience and will-power and much rubbing-out, he managed to produce a good enough replica to suit his purpose – so good, in fact, that when it was finished he could hardly bring himself to look at it, but had to pass it to Emilio carefully folded, and with his eyes closed.

The first, more general probe did not meet with much success. The staff and customers of the bar, so Emilio reported later that evening, had shrugged their shoulders and drawn back their scalps in the characteristic way that Italians have of expressing ignorance when it is wedded to total lack of interest. 'Boh,' they had told him repeatedly, varying it to 'Buah,' and an occasional 'Mah!' No, they had never seen a child like that hanging round the district. Not with teeth like that, per l'amor di Dio; they would well remember if they had. Perhaps the drawing was not a very faithful one. Why didn't he show them a photograph instead, they had asked with a little more interest, or else get the police to issue a proper description? Was the boy missing from home, or something?

The second probe, however, had been more promising. Much, much more so, reported Emilio pleasedly, who since he had discovered what store his friend set by them had become almost as concerned about the missing papers as Joseph himself. Un-luckily, he had not been able to interview the ticket-seller who had been on duty at the time of the accident, as he had been posted elsewhere in the interval, but he had spoken instead to the newsagent from the stall nearby. Although unresponsive at first to the drawing, the man remembered the incident well. Not only did he know Joseph by sight – 'Ah, si, the poor old foreign professor,' he had exclaimed delightedly: what a crash he had made – but also remembered that he had been carrying a large parcel under his arm when he had embarked. (You see, he always kept an eye on people's parcels and bags and things when they were browsing round the stall, he explained. Emilio would not credit it maybe, but it was amazing the number of customers who tried to filch books off him that way. Not that he had suspected the professor of a thing like that, of course, he had hastened to add.)

And then, after the accident, he had noticed it a second time: a bulky white parcel with tapes pasted all over it. If it wasn't the same one, it had certainly been one very like it. Only this time a little boy had been carrying it, and running off fast in the opposite direction. He hadn't given much thought to it at the time, but yes, come to think of it, it could easily have been the very same parcel. He shook his head in disapproval: nothing was safe nowadays. Fancy stealing from a poor old man who had fallen down. Would Emilio be so kind as to let him have another look at the identikit?

When Emilio brought the drawing out again he had studied it carefully, willing to collaborate in bringing a thief of any age or description to justice, but admitted with reluctance that he couldn't say for sure. The child had been dark, though, like this one. That he did remember. But he hadn't seen enough of the face to be able to identify it in the sketch. 'I'll keep my eyes open, though, for the little beggar. You can count on that,' he had added helpfully. 'I hope you catch up with him. And please give my respects to the Professore.'

In listening to all this, Joseph became so excited that Emilio had difficulty in quietening him down. 'Try and think of the matter a little more objectively, Joe,' he urged. 'The man wasn't *that* sure. What on earth would a child want with a bundle of old papers? OK, OK, we know he hasn't taken them to the lost property office . . . just keep still for a moment, won't you . . . but that doesn't mean he isn't going to bring them back. He probably wants to bring them round himself, so as to get a reward, or something. That's more like it.' He laid a restraining hand on Joseph's arm. 'Yes, I bet that's what he'll do once he hears you're back. It's not as if it were a box of biscuits, or anything he could eat, or sell.'

Joseph, however, wasn't really following, or even listening. (And perhaps this was fortunate, seeing that Emilio's last surmise, uttered rather quietly and finished off by a cross biting of fingers, was that the child had most likely thrown the package into a dustbin.) He could not get over the fact that at last, at long last, someone else besides himself had actually seen the Catcher. So he existed after all, he thought triumphantly, breaking free from Emilio's hold and banging a fist on to the bedclothes with a force that scattered the sheets of music lying there and made Lapo jump. He existed independently and bodily, as he had always known. This confirmed it. It was the best piece of news he had heard in a long while.

That night he slept long and soundly, and woke up the next morning feeling stronger and better than he had for weeks. He rose almost springily, washed and dressed with care, had breakfast brought to him from the bar, settled his rent with the padrona, and then sat down at his desk and wrote a brief note to

Emilio bequeathing him his books and whichever of his possessions he might like to keep; adding a suggestion that the revolving-wheels might one day prove to be of a certain antiquarian value. Lastly, he folded the note and put it, together with a bundle of notes which represented his entire savings, in an envelope; addressed it, sealed, it, and stuck it with Sellotape on the lowest shelf where Emilio could not miss it. With this, he felt ready for the fray.

Taking Lapo with him, he left his lodgings and walked slowly but unhesitatingly towards the palazzo. It took him double the time it would normally have taken to reach it, and double this again to mount the stairway, but he allowed himself no pauses this time, and went slowly on towards his goal with the steadiness of one drawn by a thread. The approach, he noted, was barren now, the staircase swept and clean. No more dinghies. No rotting seagulls. Replacing, or perhaps merely blanketing, the others, a strong smell of disinfectant hung on the air. When he rounded the final landing, he saw that the door to the apartment stood wide open, propped against the draught by a broom wedged under the handle, and murmuring encouragement to Lapo, who hung back reluctantly with his coat prickling, he climbed the last short ramp and stepped inside.

He was faced by an emptiness so thorough as to reawaken his sense of bewilderment and hesitation. The place was unrecognizable. The living-room – or what had been the living-room – lay colourless and bare, the only sign that it had recently been occupied being a few rectangular patches on the walls where the posters had been hung. Everything else, from the curtain rings and picture hooks down to the electric fixtures, had been stripped from its surfaces as if sucked by a giant vacuum-cleaner, and from the sockets at floor level, in place of plugs, naked wires protruded, twisted precariously apart. The girl had been true to her word: she had left, evidently, never to return.

After a quick glance into the other rooms, all similarly desolate, he made his way to the bedroom he was seeking. Not, strictly speaking, the Catcher's bedroom (although that was still how he thought of it), but the poor little blond child's bedroom:

likely annexe to the Catcher's hide-out, and to the torture-chamber of the cats.

In contrast to the others this room was not empty. Not that it was in any way furnished or decorated, either, but on a chair by the window an old man sat reading a newspaper. He started violently as Joseph appeared in the doorway, and the chair rocked beneath him, very nearly expelling him from the seat. Joseph started, too. Then, noticing a pail and mop in the corner and realizing that he had come unawares upon some cleaner or caretaker, he smiled weakly and apologized for the disturbance.

The old man placed a hand on his chest and opened his mouth soundlessly; he had evidently suffered a severe shock.

'Not for rent or for sale,' he said breathlessly when he had managed to get his voice back. 'And no journalists either, or sensation-hunters.' 'Via! Via!' he added crossly, when he saw that Joseph had not moved from the doorway, fanning the newspaper first under his own nose and then, more menacingly, at Joseph himself. 'Via. Off. Be off with you.'

On learning, however, that his visitor was from the pensione opposite, and what was more that he had known the family personally, his manner changed, and perching himself on the window-sill in order to vacate the chair in favour of Joseph – treating him, that is, no longer as an intruder or potential time-waster but as a guest and a welcome diversion, preferable even to the newspaper – he began to speak, unprompted, about the recent excitements that had taken place in the building of which he was in charge.

'Yes, they've upped sticks and gone,' he confirmed with a grave nod of the head to each corner of the room, 'and I don't blame them, either. First the husband, then the child. They say he'll get over it, mind you – and I hope they're right – but if I'd been the mother I'd have done the same: I'd have got right away from the place and you wouldn't have seen me for dust.'

He nodded again several times before launching into the narrative proper, prefacing it for Joseph's benefit by the proud announcement that he had been the one who had first noticed that there was something seriously wrong with the child, and then went happily ahead with an account of stretcher-bearers and doctors and his own prowess in holding the fort against journalists when the meningitis scare had gained momentum.

Joseph listened attentively, and still more attentively looked around the room. On noticing a dwarf-size door on the far side, though, papered uniform to the walls, but with the paper slit a trifle jaggedly to provide for its opening, his attention began to waver. 'You are the caretaker here then?' he asked when the old man had finished. 'Have you lived here long? In this neighbourhood, I mean?'

'All my life,' the man replied.

'Ah,' said Joseph slowly, trying to sound as unconcerned as possible. (The enquiry might need handling carefully: he could hardly set about it by making a dive for the little door and leaving it at that. And besides, there were a number of other things that he must try to find out first.) 'Ah, well, then, perhaps you could help me out over a small matter that has been bothering me recently. If you have time to spare, there are one or two questions I should like to ask you. About the house, I mean.'

From the way the man's face lit up as he said this, he could tell, however, that prudence was not going to be necessary. Reminiscence was clearly a favourite pastime of the caretaker's, and one he went in for diligently and without reserve of any kind. His dismissal of journalists and sensation-hunters had evidently not been meant very seriously. All he appeared to want from his audience was that it interject the odd murmur, and that it place its questions tactfully, at long intervals, without interrupting the flow of his own recollections. And this, Joseph took care to do.

He started the old fellow off on the subject of the alleged unluckiness of the house. It seemed a promising lead. How was it, he asked, that the palazzo had picked up its reputation for misfortune in the first place? What, apart from this last episode of the child's illness, had taken place there?

Well, said the caretaker pleasantly, shifting his backside into a more comfortable position. Well, now, let him think. Ah, yes, well, there had been the poor Signora Muzzi, for example. Now that had been a bad business altogether. It must have been round about the time of the Salò Republic . . .

And away he went with his chronicles: the Signora Muzzi; the diplomat with the erring wife; Ingenier Tobagi. The misfortunes to begin with were of an unexceptionable, almost routine nature. People had died there, of course, as people tend to do in many places, when choice no longer obtains. People had run into financial difficulties, had fallen out with each other, and, on two occasions, fallen down the stairs. And then the carabiniere had been killed, and the child had been taken ill, but that Joseph already knew.

The main episode, however, the one to which all subsequent ill-repute was originally attributed and linked, had taken place so long ago, and when the caretaker himself had been so young, that it took him some while to trace back to it. His slowness in touching upon what was, in fact, the key episode might, Joseph felt, have been due to a deliberate desire to prolong and heighten the dramatic effects of the telling, but he suspected that it was also due to reluctance. He could understand this only too well: he was himself, in part, reluctant to hear it.

Yes, the caretaker admitted after much shifting of the bottom and scratching of the head, there had been a family of foreigners living there once, and it had been then, he supposed, that it had all really begun. Emigrés. Refugees, or what have you. 'I russi', everyone had called them; the Russians. But in those days that might have meant any nationality at all. Thinking back on it, he didn't suppose they had really been Russians. 'Too dark,' he added slyly, as if his knowledge of Russians had been much modified and augmented during the interval. 'Too dark and too slit-eyed, if you know what I mean.'

Joseph, despite a sudden dryness at the back of his throat, managed a brief assent. This was it, he realized. They were on the right track now; from his throat, and his hands, which were trembling, and from the hectic beating of his heart, he could tell that he was about to hear something of terrible import. And clutching at the seat of the chair to prepare himself on the grossly physical plane at least, he listened spellbound as the story continued.

There had been the father and the mother, and a son of roughly his own age, the caretaker went on. Distant, they had been, though, as far as he could remember; never friendly; kept themselves to themselves. No one had liked them, and no one had been really sorry for them when the disaster happened – although it was the sort of thing you wouldn't wish on your worst enemy. Exactly how or why, nobody knew, but a year or so after their arrival a fire had broken out in the apartment one night and the family had been burned to death – all except for the son. It had created a great impression all round, as Joseph could no doubt imagine: Venetians being generally more accustomed to water. 'Poor wretches,' he added punctiliously, pleased at the interest his story was arousing. 'If you take a look at the walls here, outside the window, you can see that they are still a bit blackened in places. It was the fire that did it.' And he opened the window and beckoned to Joseph to observe the historic markings.

Joseph nodded weakly but did not rise. 'Tell me a little more about the boy,' he urged in a voice that was hardly audible.

The caretaker cupped his hand to his ear. 'Tell me a little more about the boy – the son,' Joseph repeated, and this time the words came out in a shout.

'Ah, the boy,' said the caretaker, shutting the window and pulling smilingly at his ear in apology for his deafness. 'The boy. Alessandro, was it? Or Alberto? Al-something. No, Alessandro. Alessandro. That's right. Well, as I said, it was a long time ago now. I don't know that I can remember much about him. He was stand-offish too, like his parents. They were nobles where they came from, or so people said. Aristocrats.' He gave Joseph a wink, loaded with political significance. 'That's why they had to run. But you wouldn't have thought so to look at them. They had a lot of books, of course, and pictures, and hangings and things like that, which I suppose was why the place went up like it did once the fire had caught – fsssch, like that, in flames. But they didn't look like nobles to me.'

He closed his eyes as if to recapture some image in his memory, then shrugged in defeat. 'Dark,' he said simply, sticking to his earlier description. 'Dark, and slit-eyed, and proud as Lucifer.' Then, as if stirred by the simile (it had stirred Joseph, too, to his greater discomfort), he snapped his fingers and went on with more enthusiasm: 'That's right. Of course. He used to come to school with us, or he did for a while anyway. Alessandro. Alessandro . . . I remember him now. Oho, yes, do I remember. I used to be a bit frightened of him. There was that game he taught us all to play, with a cat and a piece of wire. Yes, I remember him now. The others used to tease him a bit to begin with', here he bared his teeth and tapped them with his fingernail, 'because some doctor had fitted him out with a funny kind of metal thing for him to wear in his mouth. No one here in Venice had ever seen anything like it. I suppose there was something wrong with it – his mouth, I mean. But anyway no one mocked for long, that I can tell you. Alessandro, Alessandro,' he added musingly, drawing out the s's until they hissed. 'I wonder what became of him.'

He paused, frowned, gave Joseph a quizzical look, and enquired with a trace of sharpness: 'Did you know him yourself, then? Is that why you are asking?'

Joseph put his head in his hands, pressing the palms against his temples: it seemed a temporary way of preventing it from bursting. Had he known the Catcher? Well, *had* he, in any acceptable sense of the word? 'No, no,' he said in as flat a tone as he could muster. 'There is no personal interest involved. It is merely the historical side that interests me. I am a writer, you see, in a certain sense.'

'So you *are* a journalist, then,' said the caretaker with a wink, giving Lapo a kindly pat on the head, 'I thought as much.'

'No, goodness no,' Joseph put in hurriedly, 'nothing of the kind. I suppose you could call me a sort of amateur historian, although the field of my research . . .'

The custodian cut him short with a wave of the hand, and took out a crumpled packet of cigarettes from his overall pocket, offering one to Joseph as he did so. 'Makes no difference,' he said frankly, 'I like a chat, and to tell you the truth I don't much like being here on my own. Now that you know something of the place, I expect you can see why for yourself. Of course,' he added thoughtfully, 'it's not so bad down on the first floor where I live.' And with a drag on his cigarette and a comfortable sigh that seemed healthily to contradict what he had just been saying, he went back to his memories.

Joseph, who had begun to wonder amongst other things how he would ever be able to make his way down into the street again, and what he would do with himself once he had got there, listened despite himself. The cupboard, he decided, would just have to wait. First he must hear the story through to the end and try to digest its significance. The Catcher, as he knew only too well by now, existed indeed. Or perhaps it would be more correct to say that he *had* existed. But this – the degree of existence, and the unaccountable age-factor which seemed to have kept him, bottled as it were, or pickled, at the moment of childhood when the caretaker had known him – was not of particular interest to him any more. What he found much more interesting, and much more worrying somehow, was the mention of the father – the father, and the fire. He had carefully refrained from close questioning on this point, but as far as he could make out, the disaster had taken place in the same month and the same year as his own birth – perhaps, he suspected, even on the very same day. Nor was this all. The Catcher, like himself, had been a spectator at his parents' death. Like (and yet, surely, so unlike) his own parents, they had been burnt in front of their son's eyes.

The child, so the caretaker was now saying, had been deeply criticized in the neighbourhood for the way he had acted during the burning. He had been found salvaging from the flames . . . Joseph would never guess what: books, yes, *books*, just think of that . . . instead of trying to save his relatives or running for help. The more charitably inclined had put this down to his youth, of course, and to the state of shock he was in at the time; the less charitable and more cynical, to the value of the books (of such worth and rarity, said the caretaker, impressed despite himself by this detail, that at the boy's request an expert had been sent for from some museum or other, in order to value them and to arrange for their safe-keeping). Alessandro, however, had defended himself against such charges, when kindly informed of them by his schoolfellows, by maintaining stoutly that in so doing he had merely obeyed his father's dying command: the books at all costs were to take precedence over the humans. This, said the custodian, was very likely true. The boy had been cruel and haughty, maybe, but he had never lacked bravery. And the father, from what he remembered, would have been a hard man to disobey. Pity more didn't come back to him about it all, seeing that Joseph was so interested, but there – it had all been so long ago.

With a sigh he reached for another cigarette, and ran it under his nose with his eyes shut. And then there had been the other tenants, of course, he went on; some very nearly as unlucky. Poor Signora Muzzi and her friend, to name just a couple. Did Joseph want to hear the details of that story too, or had he already been into them? But having repeated the question twice over, without getting so much as a murmur of encouragement from his listener, he opened his eyes again and gave him a quizzical once-over, bringing them to rest on his face and examining it closely as if seeing it for the first time.

'Òstrega!' Was the professor feeling all right, he asked in a changed tone, getting to his feet and crossing over to the chair. Should he bring him a glass of water? Or something a little stronger – a drop of grappa, perhaps? Had he worn him out with all his talking?

In reply, Joseph could only shake his head in silence, so taken up by his thoughts as to be hardly able to hear what the man was saying. It was the identity of the Catcher's father that obsessed him most. Who had he been, he wondered, and what had been his profession? (Although he had a terrible suspicion he already knew the answer to this, at least in part.) What did the date of his death signify, and its parallel to the death of his own father? Why had he chosen to burn to death sooner than allow his books to be destroyed? What books were they? What had happened to them afterwards? Where were they now? And how did he himself fit into the picture? The Catcher had been plaguing him, and dogging and tormenting him all this time, for the testament, of course. For the magic. That much was certain. And he had most likely been doing it under orders from his father. But if the father had lived there so long ago, then he must have been after this secret of his not only before he, Joseph, had committed it to writing, but before he had discovered it; before he had become a magician; before he had even been *born*. He had not summoned the fiend himself by mistake, then; it had not tracked him down. It had always been there; watching, waiting, planning, and then waiting again. The implications of such studied and long-range strategy on the enemy's part were, he now realized, nothing short of shattering. For what it meant – what it could only mean – was that all his work, all his strivings and energy and perseverance, had been directed by some force or purpose of which he had all along been totally unaware; that he was nothing more than a kind of wretched stop-gap or instrument devised for the completion of a plan; and that the plan, moreover, was more powerful and more lasting than the single instruments it employed. The last link of the chain: that had been how he had thought of himself, that had been his acknowledged position all his working life. But what chain was it, exactly? And where did it lead? What had he been working for all these years, he wondered? (And had he been alone, he would not have merely wondered, but would have screamed it aloud.) Who, *who*, who, good God in heaven enlighten him, who was it he had been working for? He pressed his hands to his temples as he had done earlier, in the vain hope of stopping the pulsing, and tightened them like a vice. Much as he dreaded it, he knew that the time had now come to look behind the door, for if there were any answers to all these terrible questions, it would be the only place he might still be able to find them.

With an effort he pulled himself together and summoned a smile for the old caretaker, who was now hovering over him and clicking his tongue with an almost fatalistic relish; already, Joseph suspected, putting the incident in narrative form ready for future use. Not to worry, he explained faintly, he had recently been unwell, and was still subject to these short spells of giddiness; but he was feeling better already. If the caretaker would do him one more kindness, he would just like to have a little peep into that cupboard, or room, or whatever it was, over there, and then he would be getting back.

Ah, said the caretaker more brightly, evidently so relieved to hear him speak as to overlook the strangeness of the request; it was lucky the professor had mentioned that. It was the only room he hadn't dealt with yet. Wouldn't have done to have missed it out. They were going to have enough trouble reletting the place as it was. 'Only it's not a proper room, of course,' he added, 'more of a cupboard, really: a little cubby-hole,' and fitting a key from the bunch which he wore on his chest like a medallion, he unlocked the door and beckoned Joseph to follow.

No sooner had he swung open the door, though, than he staggered back without warning, spinning sideways as if he had caught a blow, slammed it shut again before Joseph could see inside, and turned an embarrassed shade of purple. 'Scusi, Professore,' he murmured. 'You must excuse me. I never thought . . . I should have got round to it earlier. But they seemed such clean people. Dio mio! Dio mio!' And, groping his way towards the chair that Joseph had just vacated, he sank down on it, retrieved his newspaper, and began fanning himself rapidly.

Joseph watched him, horrorstruck. He had not got that near himself, but he had smelt it all the same, and so had Lapo from the looks of things. If he had needed any more proof, this was it. He had found Azazael's hide-out. Azazael had lived here once, when the other magician had lived here; and in the person of his son, or lackey, or whoever it was that was carrying on his work for him in the latter half of the twentieth century, he lived here still.

Filled not so much with dread, or fear, as downright indignation, he marched over to the cubby-hole, and holding his sleeve to his face, threw the door open. He hardly noticed what lay beyond in the fetid darkness, for there on the very threshold, so close to the door that he almost tripped over it, was

176

what he had most wanted to find, although not in these conditions: the blue folder of his own testament. Beside it lay the plastic wrappings with which he had protected it, hastily stripped away and screwed into a ball, and surrounding it on all sides, sheet after sheet of torn, soiled and crumpled paper: the pages of the testament itself.

Heedless of the stench, and the protests of the caretaker who was fanning himself at breakneck speed and begging Joseph to close the door again, he dropped to his knees and began sweeping the pages together, trying to make out how much damage had been done to them. Even at first glance, it was all too apparent that Azazael had had a field day. Whole sections had been torn out, and then torn again, and shredded; a sticky, brown film, filamented like a snail's trail, coating every fragment. The text did not appear to have been read, so much as chewed. Parts had been so thoroughly dealt with as to be unrecognizable by anyone but their author as written material at all. It was the safety device, though, that seemed to have been given the most pitiless treatment, and as he held in his hands the pulpy mess that it had now become, Joseph could not help remembering, a scorching lump at the back of his throat, how powerful and how dangerous he had once thought it; how proud he had been of it, and, in a curious way, how it had awed him. He could have spared himself these emotions, he now realized: Azazael – though it must have angered him from the way he had treated it – had made short work of it indeed.

Slowly, tremblingly, but working a little more systematically now that the first shock had passed, he began to transfer the sections from right to left as he identified them, and to place them, like a row of corpses, in the order in which he had originally set them down. In this way, it did not take him long to realize that the chapter dealing with his great discovery – the core of the work, his secret, and his revelation to humanity – was the only part that was missing.

With a cry of despair, he began to search again, without system this time, grappling with the mass of defaced and ravaged papers like a madman, grovelling amongst them on his hands and knees, burrowing, digging, ferreting, discarding, and scattering them about him with the fury of a predator in a nest of feathers (aided by Lapo, who, unlike his master, seemed to be enjoying this part of the proceedings immensely). Then, with another brief cry, he sank back on his heels and laid his forehead to the ground.

There was no use in prolonging the search. It was missing: the vital section was missing. As was to be expected, they had taken what they had wanted and spewed out the rest: the warnings, the explanations, the safety device, all had been spat contemptuously aside, and the nugget of gold at the centre stolen greedily away. Only, without its casing it was not gold at all, but a lethal poison. He rolled his head from side to side, pressing it into the dust. Azazael, or whoever was the chief architect of the plan, had managed things with mastery. If he, Joseph, had been their instrument, he was also their sole opponent, and now that he was aware of the fact he was too tired and too beaten to resist. For whom could he turn for help at this stage? To the scathing Trevisan? To the timid and fastidious priest? To Emilio; kind, generous, woolly-headed Emilio, who believed in progress? And what could he do? His hand that had written so copiously for nearly forty years was worthless now; he doubted it could still hold a pen, let alone copy out a message. A message to whom, anyway? And saying what?

To whom it may concern. Urgent and not deferrable. Please commence search for book or books – place and date of publication, title and author unknown – presumably situated in some Venetian library, but possibly anywhere in the world, belonging, roughly sixty years ago, to an unnamed foreign resident of Venice, long since deceased, whose nationality was presumed Russian. Only clue: refer back to newspapers of the year 1922 for eventual report on a fire which broke out at Dorsoduro [here he must add the number, the only really certain piece of information he could give] in which the owner of these volumes perished. Once traced, please destroy these books instantly.

A message like that wasn't even worth writing. No. It was really the end this time. He must go back and prepare Lapo's meal for him and then try to eat something himself, and have a little rest. That was what he wanted above all else now. Rest and quiet.

Helped to his feet by the caretaker (who, what with the smell from the cupboard, and the things he had seen inside it, and the strange sight of the professor and his dog burrowing their way through the pile of papers like a couple of truffle hounds, seemed at this point almost as lost as he was himself), he made his way down the stairs and wandered slowly back to his lodgings.

Epilogue

O N THIS melancholy note, and in these melancholy surroundings (the rain has started up again, or started down, and the wind is blowing hard, as it was in the beginning), the story comes to a technical end. It is a melancholy story, anyway, and comes therefore to a fitting end, and none too soon. It may be worth a passing mention that the city throughout had been unaffected by all these shady goings on. Venice has seen stranger things over the centuries, and has harboured more unfortunate beings than a sick child, a handful of tortured cats, and a dead magician. She has seen war, and treason, and pestilence, and the onslaughts of industrialism, and if these have not managed to undermine her poise (although the last is still having a good try), then why should the characters of a mere fantasy?

Yes, I said a dead magician, for Joseph W. Kestler died (peacefully? I wonder) in his bed on the very afternoon of the day we last saw him. It was Emilio who found him. He was lying, curled foetus-wise, under the blankets, his hand still clutching a stub of pencil, a blank sheet of paper on the floor beside him. The official cause of death was lung haemorrhage, and neither Emilio, who had reluctant and ample opportunity to notice the state of the bedlinen, nor anyone else, saw reason to question it. Their only surprise, in fact, was that Joseph should have held out as long as he did.

It might occur to those who have seen something of the extent and efficacy of his strange powers, that his end was self-induced;

the foetus position suggesting that he may have rolled himself up in a ball, and, with a last and highly successful attempt at cabalistic meditation, have sought the gentle 'mors osculi', the death of the kiss, in which the highly trained cabalist calls on his own self, and is rewarded in this fatal meeting by a blissful end of his worldly troubles. Given the tenacity and moral fibre of the subject, though, this does not seem likely. It might even seem possible (but again only to those who are familiar with them) that a different set of powers stepped in and put an end to his struggles for reasons of their own. The only evidence for this, though, is a pencil and a piece of blank paper, which could just, I suppose, be taken as a sign that he was trying to write out a message, or denouncement of some kind, and was forcibly prevented from doing so; and you can't rest much of a case on that. No, I think that when the evidence is gathered and weighed, these forms of mysterious suicide and still more mysterious murder can be ruled out, and we may fairly confidently say that Joseph Kestler – occultist, theurgist, reincarnated sorcerer, or dotty old fool that he may have been – died as he lived, of natural causes alone.

In the interests of cheerfulness – a quality we have almost lost sight of in the last few chapters – I will spare you the details of Lapo's behaviour at the side of his master's coffin (those who are interested can refer back to the saga of Keret), and make scarce mention of the modestly attended funeral. Emilio was chief mourner, and – apart from a smile when he noticed that the funeral barge was preceded by another, piled high with sacks of rubbish for disposal, and thought to himself how droll Joseph would have found this, and how he too would have smiled his quaint little lop-sided smile had he only been able to see – he chiefly mourned. There is little else to be recorded. Joseph had made tidy preparations for his departure, and had severed what ties he had had, in so far as he was able. That the break wasn't a totally clean one where the dog and the student were concerned, and that a subdued and pink-eyed Trevisan turned up for the burial (as, in fact, did most of the people who had had close personal dealings with Joseph of any kind: landlady, barman, people he had worked for as an interpreter, and even one of the nurses who had looked after him in hospital), are facts that go to his credit rather than otherwise.

His familiarity with revolving-wheels, which as we have seen were part of his stock-in-trade as a cabalist, had evidently taught him to recognize in good time that the wheel of his own life had come its full circle. And there again, that it was not quite the smooth, round shape he had striven to trace, and that the final tract in particular, where the end joined up with the beginning, was an unsightly squiggle resembling a snake or a hurriedly drawn question mark, was no fault of his own.

Perhaps, though, there is one further event which deserves mention, if not for intrinsic interest, for the fact that Joseph himself would have attached great importance to it – although it would scarcely have pleased him. Three days after the funeral, an out-of-season tourist visiting a monastery not far from Venice (the exact location of which cannot be given, for reasons that are at the same time obvious and extremely obscure; suffice it to say that it was not the monastery Joseph himself had in mind) was taken ill in the library there. Well, not ill exactly, but queer. A sudden fit of dizziness came over him and he had to be helped to a chair by the monk who was guiding the visit, and revived with aqua vitae. When he recovered strength enough to speak, he explained, not without a certain huffiness, that it had been the smell that had got him: he had been standing close to one of the shelves when all of a sudden he had smelt this terrible smell – or 'goddawful stink', as he termed it – that had seemed to waft out at him from the bookcase, and had overpowered him – quite literally – by its strength.

With much unrewarded sniffing on the monk's part (for the tourist refused to take any further part in the search himself), and with a subsequent apology from the tourist (which the monk accepted rather gracelessly, seeing that there was no smell involved, and he held himself quite rightly upset about the accusation), there the episode ended. Later in the day, however, assailed by doubt or scruple or plain curiosity, the monk went back to the imputed shelf to have another look, and yet another

182

sniff. Sure enough – he had to admit it this time – there *was* an unpleasant odour coming from the bookcase. Using his handkerchief, and holding his breath, he pulled out three or four volumes and peered into the space behind, thinking, no doubt, to find some object there – a dead mouse, maybe, or lizard, or a forgotten sandwich – responsible for the disturbance. But although he looked carefully and long there was nothing to be seen. Protected by the handkerchief, his hand groped further. Still nothing. With a shrug, he made to replace the volumes. As he put back the last, however, his nose crinkled, and he drew the book out again, bent close to it, and inhaled. Then he breathed out again rapidly and put the handkerchief to his face. So *that* was what it was: it was the book that smelt. Not strongly, not overwhelmingly as the impolite tourist had tried to make out, but . . . yes . . . sharply and definitely all the same. Funny, he thought, it must be the damp. Of course, that was it; there was a small patch of mould on the cover. He must mention the matter to the chief librarian and see about giving the shelf a good airing. He rubbed the cover lightly with his handkerchief, revealing the single word 'Zapoved' in faded gilt lettering, and flicked incuriously through the pages. The text was handwritten in Cyrillic script – not a very old volume, he judged, but oldish. A hundred years old, maybe; maybe less; and, apart from the mould spot on the binding and a faint singeing of the papers at the edge, in good condition. He read the opening lines.

I, Yosif Karimov, leave these papers in the hands of my trusted disciple [here there was a space, in which someone had pencilled lightly, 'But what will his name be, I wonder? Presumably they will use the traditional initials?'] confident that they will reach through his agency none but the most attentive and sympathetic reader. I write, therefore, as if addressing in the person of the future reader another close and trusted friend, whose friendship a mere discrepancy in time has prevented me from enjoying. First, a little – a relevant minimum – about myself.

Touching, thought the monk, although personal reminiscences of obscure men were not quite his line in reading; and he riffled further to see how far the damp had penetrated. Curious, though: towards the end there was a section of much newer pages written half in Roman letters and half in some odd sort of cuneiform. The ink here was quite different. It looked . . . although it couldn't be, of course . . . yet it certainly looked like Biro. Modern pages in an antique binding? Surely not. Perhaps, then, the work was not as old as it seemed. He checked the date on the flyleaf: no, it was genuine enough and had been in the library a long, long time. Somebody had been scribbling in it, then. That's what it was. Some unauthorized person had been tampering with it. He tutted crossly. People had no reverence for books nowadays. He must warn the librarian to keep a better watch on things when visitors were around, and not to go unlocking the shelves unless there was a written permit from the Abbot for him to do so. That should put an end to such incidents. He patted the cover gently and gave a smile: anyway, he thought more comfortably as he popped it back on the shelf and turned the key, what with a good airing, and a few simple precautions, it would be quite safe now. Quite, quite safe. It didn't look a very inspiring sort of work, but – who could tell – somebody might need to consult it someday; and what better place for it to remain until that day came?

The definitive novel about the legends, the peoples and the
political realities of South Africa –

WINNER OF THE WHITBREAD AWARD FOR FICTION

KRUGER'S ALP

CHRISTOPHER HOPE

KRUGER'S ALP is the story of the priestly renegade
Theodore Blanchaille, and of his search for the missing
treasure taken out by the Boer leader Paul Kruger. For
Blanchaille, it is a journey of revelation through an exotic
landscape peopled with spies, terrorists, traitors, patriots and
exiled presidents – a journey in which betrayal, disillusion and
vicious assault lie in wait for him.

'A boldly-conceived, highly original novel . . . with a final image of
shattering impact.' *Guardian*

'An extremely attractive book – witty, fast-moving and densely
imagined . . . a considerable talent.' *Sunday Times*

ABACUS FICTION   0 349 11715 2   £2.95

THE GLAMOUR
CHRISTOPHER PRIEST

All Richard Grey wanted to do was recover, to return to normal. For four long, painful months he had been convalescing after the horrifying injuries that he sustained when a car bomb exploded near him.

He could remember the years he spent as a cameraman, covering stories all over the world, and he could remember taking a break from his career – but there was a profound blankness where his memory of the weeks before the explosion should have been. It was as if his life had been re-edited and part of it erased.

But then Susan Kewley came to visit him and she spoke of those weeks. And what Richard wanted most was a glimpse of what that time had held for the two of them. But the glimpses he was afforded took him into a strange and terrible twilight world – a world of apparent madness, the world of 'the glamour' . . .

Christopher Priest's rich and subtle narrative is mesmerising and deeply moving, as compelling and deceptive as a Hitchcock film.

'One of our most gifted writers.' *John Fowles*

'A bizarre and intriguing book.' *Guardian*

ABACUS FICTION   0 349 128103   £2.95

The No 1 Bestseller

HAWKSMOOR

PETER ACKROYD

WHITBREAD NOVEL OF THE YEAR

WINNER OF THE GUARDIAN FICTION AWARD

"A brilliant achievement, funny and horrible in turn" James
Fenton,
The Times

"With consummate formal control, he has created a
fictional nightmare, combining the genres of thriller, ghost
story and metaphysical tract . . . Its nastiness illuminates
modern evil as well as testifying to the author's brave way
with the unspeakable" Marina Warner,
Sunday Times

"Mr Ackroyd is a virtuoso writer whose prose is a
continual pleasure to read . . . An unfailingly intelligent
work of the imagination"
New York Times

0 349 10057 8   FICTION   £3.95

Also by Peter Ackroyd in Abacus:
T. S. ELIOT
THE LAST TESTAMENT OF OSCAR WILDE
THE GREAT FIRE OF LONDON

The Periodic Table

'One of the most important and gifted writers of our time . . . an extraordinary and fascinating book'
Italo Calvino

'We are always looking for the book it is *necessary* to read next. After a few pages I immersed myself gladly and gratefully. There is nothing superfluous here, everything this book contains is essential. It is wonderfully pure, and beautifully translated'
Saul Bellow

'I was captivated, but also knew that no words of mine would do this book justice. Nominally it is prose; in actuality, it is a narrative poem of magical quality'
Frederick Dainton,
NEW SCIENTIST

'This is an extraordinary book, eccentric in construction, protean in genre, grandiose in its intellectual ambition, and profoundly moving in the delicacy and depth of its engagement with tragedy'
SUNDAY TIMES

'One of the most important Italian writers'
Umberto Eco

0 349 12198 2   ABACUS FICTION   £3.95

The debut of an enormously gifted writer

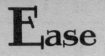Ease

■ P A T R I C K   G A L E ■

Domina Tey is one of life's success stories: an award-winning playwright, living with an equally celebrated writer in a magazine-featured home. A lucky woman, who knows and appreciates it. But at the moment, she's just not happy.

Convinced that a spell of seedy living – so far denied her by fate and circumstance – would give both work and soul a much-needed spring-clean, she elopes with her typewriter in search of la sleazy vita – discovering it in Bayswater's tarnished bedsit jungle. Within a week she has settled into the warm friendly world of Lady Tilly (landlady and ex-mortician), all-night sauna 'clubs' and midnight snack-land; and her search for a fresh start becomes an overwhelming desire to make passionate love to a much younger man. Quintus disturbs her. He's too innocent for such suffering. Domina watches his guilt changing shape, volume, direction, transforming him. Observing her, he carefully eases her out of her distress.

ABACUS FICTION   0 349 11400 5   £3.50

Patrick Gale's THE AERODYNAMICS OF PORK is also available in Abacus.

TIME AFTER TIME

Molly Keane

The ageing, one-eyed Jasper Swift and his three grotesque, elderly sisters, April, May and Baby June, have been waging quiet guerilla warfare against one another for years. They live together in damp, decaying Durraghglass, the country estate left to them all by darling Mummie.

Then, suddenly, their long-lost cousin returns from Vienna. Exotic Leda, whom Daddy had been so funny about all those years ago; and within days, the uneasy existence of the Swifts has been dramatically overturned, when desires, dormant for so long, flame fierce and bright as ever . . .

Poignant and hilarious, controlled yet outrageous, TIME AFTER TIME brilliantly captures the graceless setting of the sun on the eccentric Anglo-Irish aristocracy, emulating the classic comedy of Molly Keane's acclaimed novel GOOD BEHAVIOUR.

'Vivid and graceful . . . it is a joy to read.' *Spectator*.
'Sharp, deadly and irresistibly funny.' *Daily Telegraph*.
'The pleasure in grotesqueries is as gleeful as ever.' *Observer*.

FICTION   0 349 12076 5   £2.95

Also available from ABACUS paperback: